Also by Mary McHugh

*Available from Kensington Publishing Corp.

Cancans, Croissants, and Caskets

Mary McHugh

KENSINGTON PUBLISHING CORP.
http://www.kensingtonbooks.com

KENSINGTON BOOKS are published by

Kensington Publishing Corp.
119 West 40th Street
New York, NY 10018

All Kensington Titles, Imprints, and Distributed Lines are available at special quantity discounts for bulk purchases for sales promotions, premiums, fund-raising, and educational or institutional use. Special book excerpts or customized printings can also be created to fit specific needs. For details, write or phone the office of the Kensington special sales manager: Kensington Publishing Corp., 119 West 40th Street, New York, NY 10018, attn: Special Sales Department, Phone: 1-800-221-2647.

Kensington and the K logo Reg. U.S. Pat & TM Off.

ISBN-13: 978-1-61773-363-5
ISBN-10: 1-61773-363-6
First Kensington Mass Market Edition: September 2015

eISBN-13: 978-1-61773-364-2
eISBN-10: 1-61773-364-4
First Kensington Electronic Edition: September 2015

10 9 8 7 6 5 4 3 2 1

Printed in the United States of America

To Paris, my favorite magical city

Chapter 1

Bonjour, Paris

Why we decided to arrive in Paris on the fourteenth of July, one of France's biggest holidays, I'll never know. We call it Bastille Day because it's the anniversary of the day in 1789 when the French stormed the prison, the Bastille, to liberate the political prisoners and to celebrate the unity of France, but the French call it La Fête Nationale or *le quatorze juillet*, which just mean "The National Holiday" or "the fourteenth of July." It's a day of parades and closed shops and picnics, and fireworks at night. A day when all of France has a huge party. Kind of like our Fourth of July. A lot like our Fourth of July.

I'm Janice Rogers, and I'm going to tell you the story of our Paris adventure, which took me and my four best friends down the beautiful Seine River and into the heart of a murder mystery that we ended up solving—but not without some danger.

We were hired to dance for seven nights on a dinner cruise on a Bateau Mouche, one of the sightseeing boats that allow visitors to view the beauties of Paris from the Seine River. It would have made sense to come at least one day before the fourteenth, but Tina Powell, our leader, couldn't get a flight for the five of us Happy Hoofers until the evening before, and since Paris is six hours ahead of us, we arrived early the morning of the fourteenth.

Before we left, Gini complained that we wouldn't have time to rehearse, but Tina reassured her. "We know what we're going to do," she said. "We've rehearsed it enough. All we have to do is show up and dance. Everybody will be too full of wine to notice if we make any mistakes anyway. And we'll be part of one of France's biggest celebrations."

We believed her. What did we know? Who thought before the night was over and the last firework burst into the Paris sky that someone would be dead? Who thinks of murder on the biggest, most joyful holiday in all of France, on Bastille Day? Excuse me, La Fête Nationale.

This was my first return to Paris since my honeymoon with my second husband. It was still the same magical city it was twenty-five years before. No matter what they do to Paris, it never loses the beauty and charm that makes it different from all other cities in the world.

"There it is," Gini said, her voice almost a whisper. "The good old Eiffel Tower. We're in Paris. My Paris. I can't believe we're here."

The five of us Happy Hoofers were loaded into a van on our way from Orly Airport to the apartment we had rented for a week on Boulevard du Montparnasse, on the Left Bank, while we danced every night on the Bateau Mouche. I was glad we were going to be in an apartment instead of a hotel, because I thought it would be more relaxing.

For Gini Miller, it was a real homecoming. She studied photography for a year in Paris after she graduated from college. Whenever anyone mentioned France or French anything, her face radiated a glow that told us exactly how she felt about this city. "It was a year when I could improvise my life, Jan," she once told me. "I time-stepped my way through that City of Light, drank sweet vermouth with a twist at the Select café with artists and writers and actors and directors and . . ." She paused for breath. "I was in love with someone different every week." She became an award-winning filmmaker because of what she learned in this incredible city.

"Does all this bring back memories, Gini?" I asked.

"Wonderful memories, Jan," she said.

I love Paris too, but my view of it is slightly marred by the memory of my second husband, Derek, who wasn't all that great after the honeymoon. He spoiled Paris for me because I couldn't help thinking about the way he turned out when we got back home. That marriage only lasted two years, definitely two years too long.

"Look," Mary Louise Temple said, pointing to the glass pyramid we were passing. "The Louvre."

"We have to go there," Pat Keeler said. "There's a fantastic exhibit of Renaissance sculpture. Denise said we absolutely must not miss that."

"We're going to see everything," Tina, our planner extraordinaire, said. "I've got a list."

"Are we dancing every night?" I asked.

"That's the plan," Tina said.

"Look," Gini said, her face reflecting her delight. "There it is—the Arc de Triomphe. That's Paris personified. We're on the Champs-Élysées. Tina, I love you forever for getting this gig for us. How did you do it anyway?"

"It was the publicity about our gig on that train in Spain that landed us in all the papers because the talk show host who was murdered was so famous. We got offers from everywhere. I'm glad we decided to stick with performances closer to home during the winter. But when this offer came in, it seemed like the best one for a midsummer getaway."

"Where else could we have gone?" I asked.

"Camden, New Jersey, or Winnipeg," Tina said, trying not to smile.

"Tough choice," Pat said.

The taxi moved along the busy wide avenue. People were lined up four and five deep on either side.

"What's going on?" Gini asked the taxi driver in French.

"Madame, c'est le quatorze juillet," he said and, in French, explained what was happening to her.

Gini translated his words for us. "It's Bastille Day," she said. "They're going to close down the Champs Élyseés in an hour because of the parade. People have been waiting there since early this morning."

We passed The Gap, Disney, Hugo Boss, Sephora, and Cartier along the crowded sidewalks. There was even a McDonald's. I'll never get used to a McDonald's on Paris's most glamorous, elegant avenue.

We crossed the Pont Neuf onto the Left Bank, the artistic, bohemian part of Paris. The cafés were all crowded. The red, white, and blue French flag flew from every building. We drove down a narrow street past the Sorbonne, past the Jardin du Luxembourg, to Boulevard du Montparnasse. Everywhere we saw flowers in ceramic planters, graceful shade trees, and people walking dogs that looked clean and well-trained.

"There's La Coupole," I said, pointing to the red awning that was almost a block long. "Hemingway's restaurant. Can we eat there?"

"Of course," Tina said. "It's only a block from our apartment. See. That's where we're going to stay. The one with the balconies overlooking the boulevard."

"I lived right next door when I was here," Gini said. "That's my café across the street. The Select. I practically lived there. It's just the same."

She was almost dancing in her seat in the van. The rest of us had been to Paris once or twice, but it didn't have the same meaning for us as it did for Gini. I envied her having lived here.

Tina paid the driver a bunch of euros, and we dragged all our bags and assorted belongings to the door of our new temporary home. Tina punched in the entry code and held the door for us as we filed into the foyer. Another code opened the inside door, and we squeezed into the glass elevator that went up to the third floor.

There was one other apartment on this floor. Tina stuck the key in the door of our flat and, after some maneuvering and pulling and pushing, opened the door.

We had only seen pictures online of this place, but it was perfect. It had a large living room with a couch that converted into a bed, several big black, comfortable-looking leather chairs, a coffee table, a basket full of books in English—nice touch—a TV, and a dining table. Off the living room, there was a roomy, bright kitchenette with a combination washer-dryer, a dishwasher, fridge, stove, two sinks, and cabinets with glass doors full of plates, glasses, and serving dishes. There were two bedrooms, a room with a toilet, and a room with a shower and sink and heated towel racks, complete with thick, terry towels. In France, the toilet and the shower are usually in separate rooms.

I could have used another shower stall, but this was Paris. I was grateful for one. We'd just have to bathe in shifts. One bathroom was the only thing particularly French about this apartment, except for the view from the little balcony on one side of the living room. That was spectacular. We could look down on Boulevard du Montparnasse and watch people sipping coffee at the Select across the street, men and women hurrying by on their way to work, cars going by. Very Paris.

The view from our bedrooms was of other apartments close by. So close, in fact, that we kept the blinds down when we were dressing or running around in our underwear. The blinds opened and closed with a remote control, which took some getting used to, but they were fun.

"What do you think, gang?" Tina asked. "Are we OK with this?"

"Who gets to sleep in the living room?" Pat, our practical, always thinking, family therapist asked.

"Any volunteers?" Tina asked.

"I'll sleep in here," Mary Louise said. "I don't mind." She's our peace-at-any-price Hoofer. We all love her and take advantage of her good nature all the time. She doesn't seem to mind, so we keep doing it. People treat you the way you let yourself be treated, I've discovered in this life as an actress, director, wife, and mother.

You wouldn't think it to look at me, but I'm tough. I had my daughter when I was seventeen, divorced her father a year later, and supported my child as a waitress while I auditioned for acting jobs in New York. I'm blond with a little help from my hairdresser. People tell me I'm beautiful, but I don't really believe them because my mother never missed a chance to tell me that I was "average-looking" when I was growing up. She thought telling me I was pretty would spoil me.

My father was too busy chasing after other women to pay much attention to me. Before he left my mother for a younger woman when I was twelve, he would occasionally take me to movies and baseball games at Yankee Stadium. I adored him. I guess I've been looking for him ever since, through three marriages and countless love affairs.

My daughter and I have had some rocky times, probably because she felt neglected during her childhood. She didn't talk to me for a long time, until last year when she asked me to collaborate on a book with her about the Gypsy Robe on Broadway, a tradition among chorus dancers where at the opening of every new musical in New York, the robe is passed on to the dancer who has appeared in the most shows on Broadway. I cherish my time with my daughter.

Gini and I unpacked in the bedroom we would share. I plopped down on one of the beds to test it. It had the kind of firm mattress I like. There was no dresser, just a stack of baskets to keep our things in. No closet either. We would have to hang our clothes in the closet by the entrance door to the apartment. The mirror was weird—sort of wavy and distorted—but I checked and there was a good one in the bathroom and a full-length mirror in the living room. Not great, but you can't have everything.

I was grateful that I would be sharing a room with Gini. I like her. She always says what she means. That can be like a kick in the stomach at times, but I prefer her directness to Mary Louise's attempt to find sunshine in every disaster that comes our way. I love Mary Louise dearly, just like I love our whole gang, but I need a rest from her sometimes.

Tina and Pat shared the other bedroom. It was almost as bare-bones as ours, but there was a dresser and a mirror that you could actually see yourself in. Tina gets along with everybody. That's why she's our leader. She's the travel editor at a bridal magazine and is the most organized of all of us. She's the best one to deal with Pat's never-ending search for flaws in every situation. Pat's philosophy is that if you find things that need to be fixed ahead of time and fix them, you'll never have any problems. I don't think life works like that. Half the time, disasters that you think are going to happen don't happen, and even if they do, they're never what you expected. They just land on you with a thump, and you figure out what to do then. You improvise. Maybe because I'm an actress, I'm pretty good at improvising.

It was ten in the morning in Paris, but my body clock was still back in New Jersey and set at four a.m. I was jet-lagged. I conked out on the twin bed in the room I shared with Gini. The last thing I saw before I drifted into sleep was the framed historic map of Paris hanging on the opposite wall. *Oh, you beautiful city,* I thought. *For one week you are mine.*

* * *

We woke up ravenously hungry and headed across the street to the Select café for omelets and coffee or tea—and hot chocolate for me. Paris bustled by us on this glorious morning in July.

"What time do we dance tonight, Tina?" I asked.

"At eight-thirty, but we have to check in at our bateau this morning and find out who's in charge, what kind of music they have, what else we have to do," she said.

Well-fed and fairly presentable-looking, we headed for the nearest Metro station. "Let's get a carnet," Gini said.

My French is limited to "oui," "non," "bonjour," "combien?" and "Ou est la toilette?" so I asked Gini what a *carnet* was.

"A booklet of Metro tickets instead of one ticket at a time," she said. "It's much cheaper."

We checked the map for the nearest stop to our boat, bought *carnets*, and jumped on the Metro car that had just arrived. It was a lot cleaner than the subways in New York, but then, what isn't? It was also a lot easier to find our way because of the easy-to-follow maps everywhere in the system. I love New York, but the subway system could use a lot of help.

Our Bateau Mouche was anchored a short distance from our Metro stop. It was a long, sleek boat with glass windows all around the lower portion and an open deck at the top. Several other Bateaux Mouches were anchored in front of it. The river teemed with other sightseeing boats gliding by during the holiday week in Paris.

"Bonjour," the woman behind the ticket desk said. "Je regrette, mais il n'y a pas un bateau cette après-midi."

Even those of us who don't speak much French understood that she was telling us there was no tour that afternoon.

Gini explained to her in French that we were looking for Henri Fouchet, the person in charge of the bateau. That we were the Happy Hoofers, the entertainment on the dinner cruises for the coming week.

The woman pointed to the ramp leading to the boat and told us to ask for Monsieur Fouchet when we boarded.

We could hear the music as we walked onto the boat. Waiters were setting up the tables lining both sides of the boat, each one next to a floor-to-ceiling glass window so the passengers could see the monuments in Paris during the evening cruise. Each table had red, white, and blue flowers. Stuck in the middle of the bouquet was a little French flag with its wide blue vertical stripe on the left, a white band in the middle, and a red one on the right. There was a stairway leading from this enclosed part of the ship to the open deck on top.

"Bonjour," one of the waiters said to us as we made a couple of twirls in time to the music we could hear from the prow of the bateau. You couldn't help it. I couldn't, anyway. It was an Edith Piaf song, "Padam, Padam, Padam," the beat so strong you had to move your body along with it. I was really getting into it, when Tina put her arm around my waist and led me toward the prow. "Save it for later, Jan," she said.

Four men were sitting on simple wooden chairs. One played a trumpet, one a cello, one was on keyboard, and the other on drums. They segued into a lively version of "New York, New York" and played even louder when they saw us. We linked arms and swung into a tap routine that showed off our bodies to their best advantage. Dancing is one of the best ways to stay in shape, and we were definitely toned. We were wearing halter tops and jeans and sandals in the summertime heat. It was our kind of music.

The men played faster and faster, and we kept up with them. Finally, with a triumphant blast of sound they ended the song and applauded us as we bowed to them.

"Bonjour," the man on trumpet said to us. "Vous êtes les Happy Hoofers de New York, n'est-ce pas?" He was in his forties, his hair rumpled, a stubble of beard on his chin making him sexy.

"Oui," Gini said. "Do you speak English? I speak French, but my friends only speak English."

"Of course," he said. "We have to know English because a lot of our passengers are from America. Welcome. I'm Jean."

The other musicians introduced themselves. The drummer was young, in his twenties, his eyes bleary. His name was Yves. "Hey," he said.

Claude, the cellist, was clean-shaven, with neatly combed, long brown hair, and dark brown eyes that looked us all over and came back to me. He saluted me and said, "Later."

While the cellist and I were looking each other over, the keyboard guy grinned and said, "Where you from?" He was a little overweight but cute anyway. He had a mischievous smile and twinkly eyes, longish hair. Something about him made me think he wasn't French.

"New Jersey," Gini said. "You're not from here, are you?"

"How'd you guess?" he said. "I was born in Brooklyn. I'm Ken."

"How long have you been here?" she asked.

"A couple of years," he said. "I'll go home one of these days. But not yet."

Looking at him, I knew he'd never go back. Once Paris gets a hold on you, you don't want to leave.

"Is Monsieur Fouchet around?" Tina asked.

"He should be here any minute," Jean said. "You want to give us an idea of what kind of music you need? They just told us you tap-dance."

"We thought we'd dance to the music made famous by different French entertainers each of the five nights we'll be here. Edith Piaf, Yves Montand, Charles Trenet, Juliette Gréco, and Charles Aznavour."

"You're really going back there, aren't you?" Jean said.

"Too far back for you?" Tina asked.

"No, most of the people who can afford this dinner cruise are old and rich," Jean said. "They come here for the music they remember from the two weeks they spent in Paris when they were young. We can play that music with our eyes closed."

"Allo," a husky woman's voice called to us. "You must be the Happy Hoofers," she said with an adorable French accent.

We turned around to see a slim, brown-skinned woman with short, dark hair and large brown eyes that dominated her face. She reminded me a little of Rihanna. She was wearing a sleeveless, flowery dress and carrying a blond shih tzu with black ears. It was impossible to guess her age. She could have been anywhere from twenty-five to forty-five. She looked so French, I expected the band to strike up "The Marseillaise."

"Bonjour," Tina said. "We are the Happy Hoofers. You must be Suzette Millet. You're going to sing while we dance, right?"

"Oui," she said. "I will do the French songs from the fifties. First night, Edith Piaf? Ça va?"

"Très bien," Tina said. "Will you do 'Les Feuilles Mortes'? That's my absolute favorite."

"How could I not do 'Autumn Leaves'?" Suzette said. She put her little dog on a chair nearby and started to sing the song that I had heard many times about two lovers who separate and their love fades away like footprints in the sand. It always makes me sad to hear that song. It did so now as I listened to a voice that was an echo of Piaf's. Strong, rolling her *r*'s, passionate.

When she finished, she said, "But that's too slow for you to dance to. How about 'Milord'? That would be perfect." She sang it, first full-voiced and Edith Piafian on the chorus, then slower and sadder for the verse. We linked arms and time-stepped and mini-grapevined to this story-song of a lost gentleman, comforted by a French woman of very little virtue but much compassion, as she invites him into her room away from the cold and loneliness. Shuffling and step-stepping, we told the story with our feet and our arms and our love of this song, so French, so Piaf.

"Great song, Suzette," Tina said. "But let's do that one second. I'd rather start out with 'Les Grands Boulevards,' if that's OK with you. I love Yves Montand—that was his song. Let's work out a program and we can practice on this stage. It's small, but big enough for us to move around on, I think."

"'Les Grands Boulevards' is absolutely parfait," Suzette said. "One of my favorites." She looked up and her whole face changed, became livelier when she saw the man who had just boarded the bateau.

"Oh, Henri. Allo, mon cher," she said. She greeted a man with dark hair and sexy eyes who kissed Suzette on both cheeks. "Ça va, chérie?" he said. He was casually dressed in a white shirt open at the neck and black pants. Except for a slight paunch, he was in excellent shape.

"Ah, the Americans have arrived, I see," he said when he could tear himself away from Suzette. "Bonjour."

"Monsieur Fouchet?" Tina said. "I'm Tina Powell, and these are the Happy Hoofers, who are going to dance on your bateau this week." She pointed first to Gini, who shook his hand and rattled off a long speech in French that seemed to please him.

"Your French is excellent, madame," he said. "Where did you learn it?"

"I studied here when I was young," she said.

His attention shifted to me. His eyes widened. "And who is this?" he asked. I detected a little too much interest in his eager expression.

17

"Janice Rogers," I said, moving back a few steps before he could welcome me to the boat with a kiss.

"Enchanté," he said, kissing my hand.

Tina had to prod him gently to introduce him to Pat and Mary Louise, who were trying not to laugh. They've seen this happen a hundred times, and for some reason, they don't resent me for it. Pat once said to me, "Your looks are a fact of life, and we get more jobs because of it. Anyway, we love you."

"We are very pleased to have you with us this week," Henri said, addressing all of us. "As you know, your first performance will be tonight, le quatorze juillet. One of our biggest holidays. We have fireworks, celebrations, songs, dancing, and we fill every seat on the Bateau Mouche on this night. You will be the perfect entertainment." His eyes fastened on me again. I thought I saw Suzette frown. She looked away quickly and hugged her little dog closer to her.

"Tiens, tiens, tiens," a low, rather growly voice said. We turned to see a woman with a face that could only be French. Her complexion was flawless, her makeup subtle but perfectly applied to show off her blue-green eyes. She had a longish nose, high cheekbones, thin lips, and an expression that said, "I am here now. Don't mess with me."

"Ah, chérie," Monsieur Fouchet said. "Come

meet our Happy Hoofers, who arrived today. Hoofers, this is my wife, Madeleine."

She did not smile, just looked at each of us, deciding whether she approved of us or not.

Tina took over in her graceful, charming way, holding out her hand to Madame Fouchet. "We are so happy to be here, madame," she said. "We love being in Paris, and we are grateful to have the chance to perform on this Bateau Mouche."

Madame Fouchet took Tina's hand and her expression softened slightly. "I look forward to seeing you dance," she said.

Tina introduced her to the rest of us. Madame paused before she shook my hand, her eyes appraising me coldly. "You are quite beautiful," she said, surprising me.

"Thank you, madame," I managed to say. "That's very kind of you."

She walked over to Suzette, kissed her on both cheeks, and patted the shih tzu. "Bonjour, chou-chou," she said, moving on to greet her husband.

"Alors, Henri," she said, "you are coming with me to arrange the flags on deck?" It was not a question.

"Mais oui," he said. "Mesdames," he said to us, "you will be here by seven tonight? The guests board at seven forty-five, and our bateau sails at eight-thirty. We tour until eleven and then anchor near the Eiffel Tower to watch the fireworks on the top deck. Entendu?

19

"We will be here," Tina said.

Madame Fouchet glanced briefly at the musicians. I thought she looked a little longer at Jean, the trumpet player, but I was probably wrong. She took her husband's arm and headed for the stairway to the upper deck.

"One more time," Ken, the ex-pat keyboard guy, said, smiling at me and swinging into "Auprès de Ma Blonde." Even I knew that meant "Next to My Blonde." Things were looking up.

Janice's Fashion Tip: Don't wear shorts in Paris unless you're sixteen with gorgeous legs.

Chapter 2

Fireworks

We worked out a routine with Suzette and the band and left the boat to explore Paris before we had to return to the apartment and dress for our performance that night.

Mary Louise and Tina headed for the Champs-Élysées and shopping. "July is the best month of the year for sales," Tina said. Gini wanted to take photos of the children riding the carousel in the Tuileries. Pat said she would find the nearest café and watch the people go by. "Don't worry, guys," she said, "I'm only drinking lemonade."

Pat hadn't had anything alcoholic to drink for about a year. We worried a little that Paris and all that wine would lure her back to drinking again, so we were relieved to hear the word "lemonade."

I wanted to go back to Montmartre to relive some of the memories of my honeymoon there with Derek. I hopped on a Metro, got off at Abbesses and walked up the steep, winding street that led to the Place du Tertre just below the Sacré-Coeur at the top.

As I climbed up that hill, I remembered the day Derek and I made the same trek when we were in Paris on our honeymoon. It was a beautiful, warm day in June. We were holding hands and stopping to kiss every few yards. We were so in love. I met him when we worked together in a play off Broadway. He seemed to be fine with my having a little girl. It wasn't until we got back home that he made it clear that he didn't want her around.

But on that day in Montmartre we were halfway up the hill when some music drifted out of an open window. I think it was "April in Paris." Derek took me in his arms, and we danced right there in the middle of that little street. We felt like we were the stars in a romantic movie. I thought we would be in love in that way forever. But I've learned that "forever" doesn't exist in my life, no matter how much I think it's going to.

On this day, twenty-five years later, I was all alone. No one to dance with. No one to tell me I was the most wonderful woman in the world. No one to kiss me and dance with me in the middle of the street. I sat down at an outdoor table at one of the cafés and breathed in the feel of Paris. I missed being in love.

"What would you like, madame?" the waiter said. He was a thin, dapper man with a carefully trimmed mustache.

"A glass of white wine, please," I said. "A sauvignon blanc. And a mushroom omelet."

"Certainly, madame," he said, smiling at me. "Right away."

I was totally absorbed in the scene in front of me. The square was surrounded by cafés and shops, with an outdoor art exhibit in the middle. I watched people poking around among the paintings, some pretty good, some not. Lots of pictures of the Sacré-Coeur, Notre-Dame, the Eiffel Tower. Souvenir paintings to take home. My table was close to the narrow path that circled the square, and I could hear snatches of German, French, English, and Italian. A man stopped at my table, blocking my view.

"Want some company?" he asked.

It was Ken, the keyboard guy from the Bateau Mouche.

"Oh, hello," I said, surprised to see him. "What are you doing here?"

"I heard you tell your friends you were coming up here, so I decided to follow you. Do you mind?"

"Of course I don't mind," I said. And I really didn't. He seemed like a good guy, and I wanted somebody to talk to. "Come sit with me." He pulled a chair over to my table and sat down next to me.

"When I saw you from across the square just now, you looked sad," he said. "Are you sad?"

"Not seriously," I said. "I was just remembering my honeymoon here."

He looked disappointed. "You're married?" he asked.

"Not anymore. I don't have much luck with husbands. But the honeymoon was great."

"How many husbands have you had?" he asked.

"Three," I said. "Either I have lousy taste in men or a short attention span."

"I know what you mean," Ken said. "I was married once."

"What happened?" I asked.

"She didn't want to live in Paris. Once I came here, I never wanted to leave. She wanted to stay in Baltimore. I kept coming back here for longer and longer visits, and finally I just stopped going home. She got a divorce. No hard feelings. She comes to see me in Paris once in a while."

"What is it about this city?" I asked him.

"It's so beautiful, for one thing," he said. "Everywhere you go, there's something that takes your breath away. And French people are so different from Americans. Their whole attitude is 'If you like me, fine. If you don't, who cares?' I love the food and playing on the Bateau Mouche." He looked at me and smiled. "And meeting you. You're so lovely. You belong in Paris."

"Thank you, Ken," I said. "I do feel at home here. One of the places I loved was a little boîte near Sacré-Coeur called the Lapin Agile. "The best musicians played there. We used to sit on the floor because it was always crowded and click our fingers instead of clapping. It was so cool. I don't suppose it's still there."

"Oh, yeah," Ken said, "it's still there. It's famous all over the world. Sort of a legend. They always have the best musicians. It's still cool. Want to go there tonight?"

"Ask me again later," I said. "Let me see how I feel after dancing."

"You got it," he said.

The waiter brought my wine and omelet, and Ken ordered a beer.

"Tell me about the people in your band and Monsieur Fouchet and Suzette and Madame Fouchet." I said. "Is there a little 'je ne sais quoi' going on with Monsieur and Suzette, or is my imagination working overtime?"

"No, your imagination is right on target. Henri is fooling around with Suzette. I think Madame Fouchet knows it and ignores it. They seem to have a whole different attitude toward cheating here. They don't take it as seriously as we do. It's just sex. As long as he doesn't screw her in public, Madame puts up with a little fooling around on the side. Besides, she's no angel either."

"No kidding," I said. "Who is she getting it on with?"

"Jean. You know, the trumpet player. I think she's more serious about him than he is about her, though. He told me she talked about leaving her husband for him."

"Isn't he a little young for her?"

"They don't care about that over here," Ken said. "Did you see that Catherine Deneuve movie? *On My Way,* I think it's called. She sleeps with a really young guy, and he says to her the next morning, 'You must have been really something when you were young.' She wasn't offended at all. I mean, it's a whole different way of looking at sex over here."

"How old are you?" I asked.

"Thirty-five," he said. "You?"

"Older," I said.

He raised his glass. "Here's to older," he said.

"Is Suzette in love with Monsieur Fouchet?" I asked.

"I think Suzette is in love with Suzette," Ken said.

"So we have stumbled into a romantic intrigue," I said. "Fascinating."

"Can't wait to see you Hoofers dance tonight. You were really terrific this morning at the rehearsal."

"Thanks," I said. I looked at my watch. "I'd better go, Ken. I've got to dress and put on a ton of makeup and get back to the bateau by seven.

I'm glad you followed me. Maybe you can show me your Paris."

"It would be my pleasure," he said.

I paid and left my keyboard guy people watching at the café and took the Metro back to our apartment.

Everyone was there except Gini, who tends to lose track of time when she's taking photos.

Mary Louise and Tina showed me what they bought on the Champs-Élysées. A black silk blouse with tiny gold buttons for Mary Louise and, for Tina, a gorgeous blue and green scarf that looked fantastic with her bluer-than-blue eyes. They were the first thing you noticed when you met her.

"Can you believe this is a Dior scarf!" she said. "It was marked down to half its original price. Even in euros, it's a bargain."

"Oh, Tina, it's gorgeous," I said. "I want one. How long is the sale going on?"

"Till the end of July, but you'd better hurry. The store was packed with shoppers. Lots of Parisians as well as tourists."

Pat was already in the shower. A good thing, since all five of us had to use that one shower.

"Are we wearing black tonight?" I asked Tina.

"Yes. The skinny, clinging long dresses that are cut down to our navels in front and up to our thighs on the sides.

"How do we get back to the boat in those things?" I asked. "Not the Metro, I hope?"

"No, no, Jan. Monsieur Fouchet is sending a car for us. Hurry up and get ready."

Pat came out wrapped in a towel and scooted into her room to get dressed.

We all managed to grab a quick shower and squeeze into our black slinky dresses, high-heeled tap shoes, and rhinestone drop earrings by the time Gini appeared, fifteen minutes before the car was due to pick us up.

"Sorry, Tina," she said. "I meant to get back sooner." She looked so happy, it was hard to believe she was even a little bit sorry.

"Fifteen minutes, Gini," Tina said. "There's a car coming for us."

"Piece of cake," Gini said and shed her clothes and camera on the way to the shower. Twelve minutes later she was clean, made up, and dressed. I could never do that.

On the dot of six forty-five, a long black limo appeared and whisked us off to the Pont de l'Alma and our bateau. The French don't fool around with time. Once Derek and I were five minutes late for a bus tour full of French people, seated and waiting to start the tour. When we got on the bus, they all made a small disapproving noise—sort of a "Tsk, tsk." We were never late again.

Inside, the boat was decorated with red, white, and blue French flags everywhere on and around the white cloth-covered tables. The waiters stopped what they were doing to admire us as we stepped onto the boat. I must admit we were pretty gorgeous that night. I love it when people, mostly men, look at us like that, as if we were the most desirable women anywhere, anytime, anyplace.

At the front of the bateau, the musicians, wearing white jackets and pants, looked almost respectable. Suzette was fluttering around, flipping through the music sheets, humming a little, practically coming out of her thin-strapped, red, very short dress. She waved to us as we approached.

Madame Fouchet was talking to a man we hadn't seen before. He was tall, good-looking in an American kind of way—you know, toned and tanned, dark-haired, gray at the temples. Somewhere in his early fifties, I'd say.

She motioned to us to join them. "The Americans have arrived, I see," she said. "Allo, Hoofers. This is Alan Anderson, who owns a nightclub in New York, which he calls the Bateau Mouche. It's a succès fou with Americans. He wants to make it even more French by stealing away our Suzette to sing there. I just told him he couldn't have her. We need her here."

"Looking fine there, Hoofers," Anderson said, shaking hands with each of us as Madame Fouchet introduced us. "I've heard good things about you."

Tina smiled at him. "Thanks, Alan," she said.

"Madame," Tina said to Fouchet's wife, "where is your husband?"

"He's up on deck, making sure everything is ready for viewing the fireworks at eleven o'clock when we anchor near the Eiffel Tower. All the guests go up there and watch. It's magnifique."

"Yeah," Jean said. "Where is Henri? He's been up there a long time. I thought he'd be back down here by now. He was supposed to OK the program."

"Oh, you know Henri," his wife said. "He's a perfectionist. He wants every detail on deck to be perfect. That's so important tonight, on this holiday."

"Maybe I should go up there and see if he needs some help," Jean said.

"No, no," Madame Fouchet said. "He likes to do it all himself. I tried to help him earlier, but he shooed me away. Just leave him alone. He'll be down here soon." She turned away from Jean and the rest of us. "I'll check the tables."

She walked back to the main part of the boat, where guests were beginning to arrive and take their seats. Mostly older people—the women dressed in long gowns and the men in dinner jackets, people who could afford this expensive evening—were escorted to their tables. Everyone seemed primed to enjoy this holiday celebration, and I was thrilled to be a part of it. I sneaked a peek at the menu for the night.

The appetizers were a choice of foie gras with a balsamic reduction and sea salt; avocado tartare with citrus and vitelotte potato chips; smoked Atlantic salmon with lemon and heavy cream; beef carpaccio, parmesan shavings, and bouquet of mesclun; and albacore tuna steak with sautéed roseval potatoes drizzled with vinegar.

For the main course you could have fillet of French sea bream with roasted peaches and seasonal vegetables; prawns marinated in espelette chilies, and a vegetable trio; slow-cooked lamb roast with a rosemary sauce; stuffed poultry tournedos with tomato mozzarella gratin; or zucchini cannelloni with vegetables, tomato, and pesto sauce.

Next you had a "duet of seasonal cheeses."

Then, for dessert, you were offered a dark chocolate tart (always my choice); iced strawberry meringue "vacherin"; yuzu cheesecake with berries; raspberry chocolate dome with passion fruit coulis; or chocolate speculoos cookies. I had no idea what half these things were—especially the yuzu cheesecake. I asked one of the waiters who spoke English what yuzu was, and even though he was rushing around making sure everything was perfect, he said, "It's a cross between a grapefruit and an orange—it's from Asia somewhere."

To accompany all this, they gave you a bottle of wine for two people, with a choice of blanquette de Limoux AOC Castel Mouche; Vieilles vignes de l'Amiral; Lussac-Saint-Émilion AOC; or Bourgogne Aligoté La Chablisienne.

I definitely planned to come back here as a passenger.

As the waiters brought the guests Kir Royales to drink while they waited for their appetizers, the boat slipped out of the harbor, smoothly gliding along the Seine past the exquisitely illuminated Grand Palais, under the Pont des Invalides, the Pont Alexandre III, and the Pont de la Concorde, where there were gasps of delight at the sight of the obelisk, the fountain, and the ferris wheel, all golden on this warm summer night.

We came out and bowed to our audience as the bateau moved along past the Louvre. The band played the first strains of "Les Grands Boulevards," and Suzette's husky voice sang of the wide boulevards of Paris with their booths and bazaars, the street vendors, so much to see, people out late on summer nights enjoying the sights and noises and joys of the most beautiful city on earth.

As she sang, we did our own tap dance down the grand boulevards of Paris. Shuffling, shim-shamming, time-stepping, high kicking, and grapevining, with some ball changes thrown in, we made that bateau our own. The dance floor at the front of the boat was just big enough for us to move the way we wanted to. We really got into it, the way we always do when the music is good and the mood sublime. Suzette's voice grew huskier and sexier as she repeated the first part of the song. Our legs kicked higher and our arms spread wider as we matched her love of Paris on this most festive of all nights of the year.

When we finished, the crowd applauded, cheered in several languages, clinked their knives against their glasses and cried, "Encore," "More," "Bravo."

We backed away until we were standing next to the band. We discreetly mopped our faces and bodies, which were shiny from dancing in 78-degree heat in a small space. Suzette accepted a glass of champagne from Claude. He pulled her closer to him and whispered something in her ear. She closed her eyes and swayed a little. I thought she was going to faint, but she straightened up, shook her head, and picked up another sheet of music.

"Want to do 'Padam' after the fireworks, Hoofers?" she asked. "That will give you enough time to dry off and catch your breath."

"That's fine, Suzette," Tina said. "But I really should check this with Monsieur Fouchet. I was sure he'd be here by now."

"He'll turn up soon," Suzette said, exchanging a look with Madame Fouchet. "N'est-ce pas, Madeleine?"

"Of course," Madame Fouchet said. "We won't be going up on deck to see the fireworks until the guests have had their dinner. He's probably just having a cigarette before he comes down. Don't worry."

The Bateau Mouche sailed slowly along the rest of the route, past the Hôtel de Ville, Notre-Dame, the Musée d'Orsay, the Palais Bourbon, and Les Invalides, all glowing golden against the night sky, as dinner was served. The waiters brought us a platter with a taste of all the courses, which were perfection.

Just as the guests were sipping the last of their coffee, the bateau stopped in front of the Eiffel Tower where the fireworks were about to begin.

Jean stepped forward, and the crowd stopped talking to listen to him.

"Monsieurs et mesdames," he said, "it is time for the pièce de résistance of our holiday cruise. Please go up on deck and take the seats that we have provided for you. The fireworks will commence in fifteen minutes."

The guests pushed back their chairs and started up the stairs leading to the open deck on top of the bateau.

When the first two people stepped onto the deck, there was a loud scream. An American woman with white hair started back down the steps. "There's a man up there," she said. "I think he's dead. There's blood all over."

Jean pushed his way through the crowd on the stairs and said, "Will you return to your seats, please, ladies and gentlemen. You will be able to see the fireworks through the windows below."

"You must be joking," the woman said. "I don't want to stay on this boat another moment. How can you talk about fireworks with a dead man lying there?" She turned to her companion, an elderly gentleman who didn't seem to understand what was going on.

"What's the matter, Elyse?" he said. "Why did you scream like that?"

"There's a dead man up there, Andrew," she said. "Let's just get out of here."

Madame Fouchet quickly reached the woman's side, patted her arm, and said in a soothing voice, "Please sit down, madame. We will be back at the dock in a few minutes, and you will be able to leave the boat then."

She clapped her hands together and said to the head waiter, "Paul, brandy for everyone, s'il vous plait."

Elyse and her husband, Andrew, returned reluctantly to their seats, as did the other passengers. The cheerful mood of the evening had vanished. Even the free brandy didn't help.

I grabbed Jean when he came back down the stairs. "What's happened, Jean? Who is it?"

He pulled me over to the side. "It's Henri. He's dead. It looks like he was shot. I've got to call the police."

He pulled out his phone and went to the front

of the boat, where he told the other members of the band, my gang, and Suzette what had happened.

Suzette didn't say anything. She just stood there looking stunned, clinging to the cellist, Claude.

Jean was dialing the police when Madame Fouchet ran over to him and took the phone away from him. She said something to him in French. He started to argue with her, but she prevailed and prevented him from dialing.

Since the whole conversation was in French, I had no idea what she was saying, or why she wouldn't let Jean call the police. From the look on Gini's face, I could tell there was something odd going on. Tina and I pulled her over to the side next to Pat and Mary Louise.

"What's going on, Gini?" Tina said. "Could you hear what she said?"

"Yeah," Gini said, speaking in a low voice. "It makes no sense. Madame Fouchet told Jean not to phone the police until all the passengers were off the boat. She didn't want them to be questioned. She said it would be bad publicity for the bateau and nobody would sail on it again."

"That's crazy," Pat said. "You mean, all these people are just going to disappear without the police talking to them to find out if they saw anything suspicious? One of them might even have killed him. It makes no sense."

"Looks that way," Gini said.

"If she's not going to call the police, one of us should," Tina said.

We all looked at Gini. "Hey, not me," she said, shaking her head.

"You have to," Tina said. "You're the only one who speaks French well enough to explain what happened."

"You're right, Tina," Gini said. "You're always right." She reached for her phone and dialed. "Allo," she said, but before she could continue, a man's hand took her phone away. "I've already called them, Gini," Alan Anderson, the American nightclub owner, said.

I was surprised to see him because I hadn't noticed him at any of the tables when we were dancing.

"Are you mad?" Madame Fouchet said to him when she realized what he had done. "You have ruined our business."

"Madeleine," Anderson said to her in low, carefully modulated tones, "they tell you your husband is lying up there on the deck, obviously murdered by someone on this boat, and you haven't even gone up there to see if it's really him. And you want to let everybody off the boat before anyone is questioned? Do you want everyone to think you put business before your husband? Or even that you might be the one who killed him?"

Madame Fouchet's expression changed from angry to chastened.

"Oh, Alan, you're right, of course. I wasn't thinking clearly. Take me up there, will you, please? I can't do it alone."

He took her hand and led her up the stairs to the upper deck just as the bateau pulled into the dock where we could see the police waiting to board her.

Chapter 3

We Are Not Amused

A woman with short blond hair wearing a police uniform was the first to enter the boat. She wore no makeup, but she didn't need it. Her face was classically beautiful, her expression serious. Alan was waiting to greet her as she stepped on board.

"There's been a murder," he said. "The body is on the upper deck. May I speak to the police captain, please?"

"You are speaking to her," she said, her tone of voice indicating her displeasure. "I am Captain Chantal," she said. "And you are?"

Alan looked embarrassed. "Pardon, madame," he said. "I am Alan Anderson, a business associate of Monsieur Fouchet, the man who was killed. My French is not very good. Do you speak English?"

The police captain gave him a look of such disdain it ricocheted off the walls.

"I studied at Oxford," she said. "You must be an American." It was obvious she did not think highly of Americans. She turned away from him and headed for the stairs to the upper deck. The other police officers followed her, and Alan was behind them. "Please make sure nobody leaves this bateau," she said to one of her men.

"They have a woman police captain in Paris?" Pat said, obviously impressed. "Things are looking up. And she's hot."

"Cool it, honey," Gini said. "She doesn't look all that friendly."

Pat gave her a wicked smile. "Maybe," she said. "Maybe not."

"What is it about us?" Mary Louise said. "One little dance and someone's dead."

"I guess the killer didn't read our contract," Tina said. "No more murders."

"It's not that funny," I said, feeling a little queasy all of a sudden.

Ken, the keyboard guy, put his arm around me. "Are you okay, kid?" he said.

"Not really," I said, grateful for his support. "Why would anyone kill Monsieur Fouchet?"

"I guess our cute little police captain will have to find that out."

"Watch it with that 'cute little captain' stuff," Gini said, her voice betraying her annoyance. "You have to be twice as good as a man to get a job like that. Don't underestimate her."

Ken looked abashed. "Sorry," he said. "I just meant . . ."

"I know what you meant," Gini said, softening a little. "It's a common mistake people make about attractive women—thinking they must not be very smart. I just get tired of hearing it all the time, that's all."

"She's coming back down the stairs," Tina said. "I wonder how long she'll keep all these passengers here on the boat. They are definitely not happy. You can hear them grumbling."

The captain was a middle-sized woman— about five feet, five inches tall, but she seemed much taller. She held herself straight, and her walk was determined. She was followed by Alan Anderson and Madeleine Fouchet. Madeleine was holding on to Alan's arm tightly, barely able to make it down the staircase. He helped her to a chair and handed her a glass of brandy. She looked as if she would pass out any minute.

The captain turned to face the seated passengers, whose hostility was patent. There was immediate silence.

"I am sorry to detain you," she said, "But, as you know, there has been a crime committed on this bateau. It is necessary to take your names and where you can be reached before you can leave the ship. We will do that as quickly as possible."

There were murmurs in the crowd as these people who thought they had paid to eat a great meal, listen to excellent entertainment, and see the fireworks on the most festive of all holidays in Paris found themselves held at midnight on a tour that now seemed a big mistake.

"Excuse me," a large man with a comb-over and a Midwestern accent said. "My wife and I are leaving Paris tomorrow morning. We have to get back to our hotel. How long are you going to keep us here?" He did not sound happy.

There were sounds of agreement at tables all over the bateau.

"Monsieur, I will release you as soon as I can," the police captain said. "I'm sure you understand that these are extremely unusual circumstances. I ask for your patience."

The man didn't look very patient, but he stopped growling.

"First of all," Captain Chantal said, "did anyone hear anything suspicious or notice anything that didn't seem quite right while you were eating your dinner?"

None of the passengers spoke up, but one of the waiters cleared his throat and said with a strong French accent, "While we were setting up the tables, I went up there—on deck—to ask Monsieur Fouchet if he needed any help. I thought maybe with the chairs. He was talking to some man. I tried to ask him if he needed me, but he waved me away, so I didn't interrupt him and came back downstairs. I kept on setting up the tables when a little while later I heard some kind of loud noise from the deck. It sounded like a champagne cork. I thought he and that man were drinking champagne because it's a holiday. If I had only gone back up there—" His face crumpled. "I should have gone back there."

"N'inquietez-vous," Captain Chantal said, putting her arm around the man's shoulder, soothing him. "Do you remember what the man looked like?" she asked gently.

"Like he was from India or one of those places over there," the waiter said.

"His face was dark-skinned?" she asked.

"Yes," the waiter said. "And he had an Indian accent."

"Please be on the boat tomorrow," Captain Chantal said. "I would like to ask you some more questions." She patted his arm and smiled at him. "And you did nothing wrong."

She waited to see if anyone else would volunteer some information, but the passengers fidgeted in their seats, anxious to leave the bateau. No one spoke up.

The captain sent her officers to each table to get names and addresses. With her iPad in hand, she turned back to our gang, the musicians,

Suzette, and Madame Fouchet. She looked intently at each one of us and then spoke to Madame, who was still in a state of shock.

"You are Madame Fouchet, the wife of the murdered man?" Captain Chantal asked. Her voice was hard. I thought she might have been a little kinder, considering the circumstances. This woman had just seen her husband's lifeless body.

Madame Fouchet winced at the coldness of the question.

"Yes," she said, "I am."

"When was the last time you saw your husband?"

"About six o'clock, he went up on deck to supervise the placing of the chairs for the passengers to watch the fireworks later on."

"Did he come back down at any time?"

"No."

"Didn't you wonder what was taking him so long to—as you say—supervise the placing of the chairs?" Her voice had a sarcastic edge to it. *Take it easy, lady,* I thought.

"I went up on deck once to ask if I could help, and he said he wanted to do it by himself. He is—was—a very independent man. He didn't like anyone telling him what to do." Madame Fouchet took out her handkerchief and dabbed at her eyes.

"What time was that?"

"About six-thirty, I think,"

"Was anybody with him at that time?"

"No, he was alone."

"And during the entertainment, the serving of the meal, during the rest of the trip, you didn't wonder why he hadn't come back downstairs?" Again the captain's tone was one of disbelief. I didn't like her. I didn't see why she was being so harsh with this woman whose husband had just been murdered.

"I assumed he had come back down," Madame said, straightening up, not one to be bullied by anyone, "but I was busy making sure the meals were served properly and checking to see if the musicians or dancers needed anything. That's my responsibility."

I shot Tina a questioning glance. She shrugged. Neither one of us could remember her checking anything with us.

Captain Chantal saw Tina's shrug. She didn't miss a thing, this one. She walked over to our group.

"Your name?" she asked Tina.

"Tina Powell."

"You are the American dancers?" she asked.

"Yes, we are, captain," Tina said. She pointed to each of us in turn and told her our names.

"Ah, yes," the captain said. "You are known as the Happy Hoofers, I believe?" We nodded. She addressed Tina again. "You seem to have some question about Madame Fouchet's statement that she checked with you to see if you needed anything."

"Oh, well, I . . . ," Tina stuttered. "She certainly may have asked us if we needed anything. We were a little nervous, and I don't remember everything that happened. This was our first appearance on the boat."

"I see," the captain said. "How did you end up dancing on a Bateau Mouche?" she asked.

"Monsieur Fouchet heard about us and hired us." Tina said. "Naturally we jumped at the chance. We love Paris and couldn't wait to get back here."

The captain managed a grudging smile at Tina.

"Will you please leave your name and a cell phone number so I can talk to all of you more tomorrow?"

"Of course," Tina said, handing her our card. "We're staying in an apartment on Boulevard du Montparnasse."

The captain turned her attention to the band. She frowned when she looked at Yves, the drummer, who was struggling to stay awake.

"I hope we're not boring you, monsieur," she said to him.

"Oh, that's all right," Yves said, a silly grin on his face. "I'm not bored."

Captain Chantal turned away from him in disgust. It was obvious he wouldn't have the energy to kill anyone.

The captain's attention fastened on Jean, who couldn't seem to meet her eyes.

"You are?"

"Je suis Jean Giraudoux," he said.

"Do you speak English?" she asked.

"Oui, Capitain," he said.

"Please do so," she said, "for the benefit of those who do not speak French."

"I will," he said, mopping his face with a napkin.

"Do you know anyone who might want to kill Monsieur Fouchet?" she asked.

Jean wiped the perspiration from his face again and said in a low voice. "No, ma'am. Everybody loved Henri. He was a good man."

The captain turned to Claude, whose arm was around Suzette. She was clutching her shih tzu, her face buried in Claude's chest.

"Did Monsieur Fouchet have any enemies that you know of?" she asked Claude.

"No," he said. "As Jean said, everyone loved Henri."

She looked at Suzette. "Do you speak English, mademoiselle?"

"Yes," Suzette said. "I'm better in French, but I'll do my best."

"If I'm not clear, let me know and I'll translate," Captain Chantal said.

"Merci, madame," Suzette said.

"How well did you know Monsieur Fouchet?"

"He was my boss," Suzette said, patting her dog.

"Did you see him—socially?"

Suzette glanced at Madame Fouchet, who looked away.

"Sometimes," Suzette said.

"Was he more than just a friend?"

"Of course not," Suzette said. "I am engaged to Claude." She snuggled closer to the cellist.

The captain looked skeptical and turned to my friend, Ken.

"You are American?" she asked him.

Ken smiled. "Is it that obvious?"

"We are not playing games here, my friend," she said. Ken was immediately serious.

"Sorry," he said. "I meant no disrespect."

The captain relented a little. "I heard you talking before. That's how I knew. There's no mistaking the American accent. Do you have any information that might help us?"

I remembered my conversation with Ken at the Place du Tertre when he told me about Jean having an affair with Madame Fouchet and Suzette fooling around with Monsieur Fouchet. I wondered if he would share this fascinating information with the captain. It did seem relevant.

"I'm afraid not," he said, his face reddening slightly. "Henri was a good man. I don't know why anyone would want to kill him. "

"So it seems," Captain Chantal said, her expression making it plain she was not fooled by any of us. "I will talk to you again tomorrow. Please be available."

With that, she rejoined her officers, who had obtained the names and addresses of the passengers and were escorting them off the bateau.

The police captain waited until all the guests had left and then said to us. "Till tomorrow, mesdames and messieurs. Please be back here at eleven o'clock."

She left, and we all relaxed.

"She's a pistol, that one," Gini said. "And there goes our morning in Paris. I wanted to go over to Notre-Dame and walk around the Île de la Cité and then go to the Île Saint-Louis."

"We'll work it out, Gini," Tina said. "Don't worry. Let's go home and get some sleep. It's one o'clock, and I'm bushed."

The car was waiting for us, and we piled in and crashed as soon as we got to the apartment.

**Janice's Fashion Tip: Work that silk scarf—
it's your best accessory.**

Chapter 4

Morning in the Garden of Eden

The next morning I woke up before the others. Gini was in a deep sleep in the other bed. When I crept out of our room to take a shower, there wasn't a whisper of sound from the other three Hoofers. I was slept out and wanted to explore early-morning Paris by myself. It was only seven o'clock, and we didn't have to be back at the bateau until eleven. I had plenty of time to walk and dream.

The others were still fast asleep when I closed the heavy front door of the apartment behind me as quietly as I could and took the elevator down to the foyer of the building. It was already very warm outside. I was glad I had on my sleeveless flowery print dress and sandals. I didn't bother with makeup, just some sunscreen, figuring I could do all that when I got back to the apartment

Where should I go? I pulled out my map of Paris. We were on the Boulevard du Montparnasse near the Rue Vavin. I traced the little street northward and saw that it led to the Jardin du Luxembourg. I remembered Gini's beautiful photographs of the garden and decided to go there. It didn't look too far to walk on this summer day, so I set out for the public park. I remembered it vaguely from my honeymoon; Derek and I had stumbled on it after walking all day exploring this incredible city. We collapsed onto a bench near the pond where children were playing with little boats with red and orange and blue and white sails. He put his arm around me, and I lay my head on his shoulder.

We watched the children for a while. I remember he said, "I never know what to say to kids." I was too much in love with him to take that as a warning that he might have a problem with Sandy, my little girl. We'd married soon after we'd met, and he hadn't seen her very often. She was either in school or asleep when we dated. It wasn't until we got back home that it became obvious he didn't want her around.

I didn't find out until much later how much Sandy resented me for marrying him. She said to me one time, "I was so lonely when you were married to Derek, Mom. I felt like you didn't want me anymore." It took me two years to realize I had to divorce him. I should have done it much sooner.

On this day, I got to the Jardin just as they were opening the tall black gates into the park. When I strolled down the path that led to the pond in front of the Luxembourg Palace, which was the French Senate building now, my whole body relaxed. Somehow this public garden breathed out a tranquillity and peace that you could feel down to your toes.

The garden was beginning to wake up. A little booth selling croissants and coffee. A man walking ponies into the park for children to ride. The workers at the Theatre du Luxembourg setting up chairs in front of the tiny stage where Punch and Judy would beat each other's heads in later on. I never got that. Why did children laugh at this terribly mismatched couple knocking each other over with bats? Why was that funny? I remembered Leslie Caron in one of my favorite movies, *Lili*, talking to the battling couple as if they were real people and begging them to be nice to each other.

On some of the chairs placed at different places in the garden, a lot of them facing the pool, there were old men, their feet up on other chairs, their heads down, dozing in the early-morning light.

Everywhere I walked there were flowers at the edge of the green lawns, around the statues, near the fountains. Pale pink tulips surrounded a small Statue of Liberty, a miniature version of our own lady who welcomes people to America. Daffodils spread their light around a beautifully sculpted Queen Anne of Austria. My guidebook told me she was married to Louis XIII at fourteen. She was a lovely queen. So lovely, in fact, the book said, that Dumas used her as a character in *The Three Musketeers*.

Red, orange, and yellow asters brightened the statue of a man with a mask pushed back on his forehead, his mouth open, his arms reaching out, his whole stance announcing his profession. He had to be an actor. I looked at the small identifying plaque, which told me that indeed he was a Greek actor.

An old man paused as he walked by, looked up at the statue, and said, "Affreux!" He was frowning. It was clear he did not like this statue. He shook his cane at the actor and kept going. I reached in my bag for my pocket French-English dictionary and found that he had called the sculpture "frightful."

I suppose I would have agreed with him if it hadn't been a statue of an actor. Instead, I felt sympathy for this Greek actor, knowing how hard acting is. Still, I love it. I'm most alive when I'm up there on that stage, absorbed in the ges-

tures, words, and emotions of another person.
For a little while, I can escape from the real world
and become someone else. Martha in *Who's Afraid
of Virginia Woolf.* Sally in *Cabaret.* Stella in *A Streetcar
Named Desire.* The wife in *Death of a Salesman.* The
mother in *The Glass Menagerie.* Sometimes I wish
I could just live on the stage all the time and skip
actual life.

I sat down on a chair near the pond and
watched people on their way to work. Women
with serious faces, men smoking cigarettes, people heading for offices. I could never do what
they do. I leaned back in my chair and felt the
sun on my face. Later on it would be too hot to
do that, so I was glad I had come out early.

The smell of coffee drifted over from a small
food stand nearby. I wished someone would
bring me a cup. I felt too relaxed and content to
get up and get one for myself.

"You're too beautiful to sit here all by yourself," a man's voice said. I opened my eyes to see
Alan Anderson, the nightclub owner from New
York, standing there. He even looked good in
the bright morning light. He was wearing a blue
sport shirt and jeans. His arms were muscled
and tan. His gray eyes were clear and focused on
me. I wished I had done something to my face
before I went out for this walk.

I sat up. "What are you doing in the Luxembourg Gardens at this hour?" I asked, pushing
my hair back behind my ears.

"I always get up early and walk in Paris when I'm here," he said. "This park is about as different from Central Park as you can get."

"What is it about this place?" I asked. "Central Park has statues and fountains and ponds too, but it doesn't feel like this at all."

"In New York you have to hustle or you'll never make it there, as they say in the song," Alan said, sitting down on the bench next to me. He even smelled good—like some expensive soap. "Here, they believe in slowing down, staying in the moment, enjoying what you have in front of you. Whether it's a woman or a glass of wine. I always say I'm going to take this feeling home with me when I go back to America, but it's no use. I rev up the minute I get off the plane."

He stopped and looked at me, not doing anything, just sitting on a bench in Paris at nine in the morning. "What are you doing here so early? Shouldn't you be practicing your dance for tonight or something?"

"I woke up early and something drew me to this park," I said. "I'm glad I did. It's so relaxing here."

"Can I get you a cup of coffee?" he asked. "I was about to get one for myself."

I smiled. "Oh, please," I said. "I was trying to get the energy to walk over there, but I didn't want to move."

"Wait here," he said and walked over to the

booth. He even looked good from behind in those tight jeans.

I liked this man. He looked like he could have been an actor.

He was back in five minutes with coffee and a warm croissant for each of us.

"How did you know I love croissants?" I asked.

"I didn't," he said. "But I don't know anybody who doesn't love them. Especially here."

I took a bite of my croissant and flaky crumbs scattered all over my lap. I brushed them off.

"Who do you think killed Monsieur Fouchet?" I asked him. I don't know why I asked him that. I hadn't been thinking about the murder at all, but it just popped into my mind, and I wanted to know what he thought.

He looked startled at the abrupt change of subject. Then he said, "I have no idea. He had lots of enemies, though."

"Why is that?" I asked. "I thought everybody liked him."

"There are people who make their living selling stuff to the Bateaux Mouches, and he always refused to buy from the right people."

"What do you mean, the right people?" I asked.

He looked at me as if trying to see if he could trust me. "People who expected him to pay more than the going rate. For protection."

"You mean, like the Mafia?" I asked.

"Yeah, right," he said. "I always make sure to

pay them in New York. Otherwise, I wouldn't last five minutes."

"You think someone killed him because he wouldn't cooperate with them?"

"I do," Alan said. "Those guys don't fool around."

Somehow he had managed to eat his croissant without being covered with crumbs. How do people do that? I felt messy and brushed at my skirt again.

"We're supposed to meet with the police captain at eleven," I said. "Will you be there?"

"I'll do my best," he said. "But I have a meeting at ten, and I'm not sure if I'll get back in time."

"That captain didn't look like she would put up with a no-show," I said.

He smiled. "There's always ways to get around a woman like that," he said.

"How do you do that?" I asked.

"Can't give away all my secrets," he said, standing up. "I'd better go. If I don't make it at eleven, I'll be there to see you dance tonight. You guys are really good."

"À bientôt," I said, pretty sure that meant "See you soon." He hurried off toward the nearest Metro stop.

I glanced at my watch. Almost ten o'clock. Time to get back to the apartment. I stood up reluctantly and started back to the open gate that led to the Rue Vavin.

* * *

Back at the apartment my friends were in various states of dress or undress.

"Jan," Tina said, "where were you?"

"Hi, Tina," I said. "I woke up early and walked over to the Jardin du Luxembourg. I loved Gini's pictures so much I had to go there."

"Isn't it gorgeous?" Gini said, a towel wrapped around her, grabbing a blouse and skirt from her bag.

"So peaceful," I said. "Oh, Tina, guess who I saw while I was there?"

"Tell me," she said.

"Alan Anderson. You know, the guy who owns that nightclub in New York who wants to hire Suzette to sing there."

"I understand she really wants to go there." Pat, who was already dressed and sipping a cup of coffee, said.

"We didn't talk about that," I said. "I did ask him who he thought killed Fouchet, and he said the Mafia, because Henri wouldn't pay the extra protection fee they demanded."

"The Mafia!" Gini exclaimed. "What did he mean, the Mafia? I didn't think they existed anymore except on that TV series *The Sopranos*."

"Don't kid yourself, Gini," Pat said. "They're mostly Albanian Mafia in Paris. They're all over the world. I was reading about them in the *Wall Street Journal* a couple of weeks ago. Very powerful."

"Didn't that waiter say he saw a man up on deck with Fouchet who sounded as if he was from India?" Mary Louise asked. "Doesn't sound very Albanian."

"Yes, he did," Tina said. "But there's no use trying to figure this out ourselves. Let's go over to the bateau and see what that police captain—what's her name? Chantal? Has to say. Are we all ready to go?"

"Let's go, guys," Gini said, picking up her camera.

Janice's Fashion Tip: Do not pack that T-shirt that says, "I don't think we're in Kansas anymore, Toto."

Chapter 5

Nothing Like a Well-Fed Shih Tzu

When the five of us go anywhere together, people stare at us. We are a good-looking bunch. Well, it's true. We carry energy with us wherever we go. It's sort of contagious. People smile when they see us. I love that. The Happy Hoofers is a good name for us because we look like we've invented joy.

A subway ride later, we were back at the bateau exactly at eleven. Captain Chantal was waiting for us. The members of the band, the waiters, Suzette, and Madame Fouchet were already there. I think to the French "on time" means half an hour early. They nodded to us as we boarded the boat. Alan Anderson had not yet arrived

"Ah, Hoofers," the captain said. "Please be seated. I'll be with you tout de suite."

Without any makeup on her face, this woman looked as if she could star in a movie about a murder on a Bateau Mouche. There was a kind of radiance about her. One by one she called each of the band members to the back of the boat to question them, then the waiters.

While the captain was talking to each of the waiters, Madame Fouchet and Suzette, holding her shih tzu, who was named Pierrot, were off on the side at the front of the boat talking to each other in low voices. Low or high didn't matter to me since they were speaking in French. Madame was wearing a pristine white pants suit. How she managed to look so wrinkle-free on this broiling July day, I'll never know. Some women just seem to do this without any effort at all. Madeleine was one of them.

We Hoofers tried to find out what the captain had asked the band but Jean and Claude were speaking to each other in French with their backs to us. Yves was swaying to music from his iPhone and smoking a Gauloise, which smelled acrid and strong. Ken was the only one who paid any attention to us. He looked rumpled and un-washed, but cheerful.

"Hi, Hoofers," he said. "Why did you do it?"

"Not funny, Brooklyn," Gini said. "Did you hear anything interesting from Jean or Claude? I don't really count Yves."

"Not really," Ken said. "They don't exactly confide in me because I'm an American. All they care about is whether I can play the keyboard. I did notice one interesting thing, though."

"What? Tell us, Ken," I said.

He lowered his voice and moved away from Madame Fouchet and Suzette. We backed up into the main part of the boat.

"Madame Fouchet and Jean arrived together," he said. "They never did that while Monsieur Fouchet was alive. Now she doesn't seem to care whether they're seen together or not."

"Big deal," Gini said. "What if they *are* having an affair? That doesn't prove anything. Nobody kills anybody here for fooling around with someone else when they're married. It's accepted. If she wants to appear with him openly, so what?"

"It's just that . . . ," Ken said. "You'd think she'd wait a little while longer. Her husband has only been dead for one day. Murdered. Shouldn't she be more broken up—or at least pretend to be? I mean, I'm divorced, but if someone killed my wife, I'd at least act sad."

"Oh, you're so American, Ken," Gini said, smiling at him.

The police captain called each of us separately to the back of the boat for questioning. After Tina, Mary Louise, and Gini answered some routine questions, it was my turn. I went back to the stern, where there was a beautiful view of the Seine and I could view the sightseeing boats passing by through the wide glass windows.

She looked me up and down. I hoped I had brushed off all the croissant flakes. I felt messy and sweaty.

"Madame Rogers?" she said.

"Yes. Janice Rogers," I said, hoping to lay the groundwork for a more friendly relationship.

She was not buying that friendship stuff. "How well did you know Monsieur Fouchet?" she asked.

"Not at all well," I said. "I met him yesterday. Tina handled all the negotiations for our appearance here."

"What did you think of him?" she asked.

"He seemed very nice. A bit of a flirt, but nice. I wish I had had more of a chance to talk to him."

"Was he here before you performed last night?"

"No," I said. "Madame Fouchet said he was on deck supervising the seating for the fireworks."

"And he never came down from the deck while you were getting ready to perform?"

"No. We assumed he had a lot of things to do up there since it was Bastille Day," I said.

"What do you think of Madame Fouchet?" she asked.

"A little cold, maybe," I said. "But I don't really know her either."

The captain leaned in, alert. "Cold? How do you mean cold?" she asked.

"Oh, you know," I said. The captain's intensity made me uncomfortable. I was just speculating about somebody I had met the day before. "She seemed only to care about the bad publicity after her husband was murdered. She didn't seem terribly upset by his death."

"Was she always on this deck after you arrived?" the captain asked.

"Yes. She was supervising the waiters, telling the band what to do, consulting Suzette."

"Consulting? What was she consulting her about?" Captain Chantal asked. She wrote something in French on her iPad.

"Maybe consulting is the wrong word," I said, a little flustered by this brusk captain. "I don't speak French, but I assumed she was going over the songs Suzette would sing and that we would dance to."

"I see," she said. "Was it your impression that Madame Fouchet and Suzette were friends. Or at least had a good relationship?"

Friends didn't seem the right word, but I wasn't sure what their relationship was.

"I'm not sure, Captain Chantal," I said. "I haven't known either of them long enough to know what kind of a relationship they had."

The captain made a couple of notes on her iPad

and then said, "Thank you, Madame Rogers," she said, standing up.

I stood up too. "Anything else, Captain Chantal?" I asked.

"No, that's it for now," she said. Then she moved closer to me and asked in a low voice, "Any chance we could see each other—alone—while you're here?"

This was so unexpected I nearly fell back in my chair. It seemed so totally unprofessional. Did she mean what I thought she meant? I never know when someone is coming on to me or just being friendly.

"Captain, did I give you mixed signals?" I asked. "I mean, what are you asking me?"

"I'm asking you if you'd like to go out with me," she said calmly, as if this was no big deal. There are some things about the French that I will never understand.

"I only get involved with guys romantically," I said. "But you might want to talk to Pat Keeler. She already said how attractive you are." Pat would have killed me if she heard me say that.

The captain relaxed. "Merci bien," she said. "Would you send Madame Keeler back here next, please?"

I ran back to our group and grabbed Pat. "She wants to meet you," I said. "And I don't mean in an official way."

"She's gay?" Pat said. "Really? Oh, this is very interesting. She's gorgeous!"

"What about Denise?" I asked, referring to the woman Pat was involved with at home. I had forgotten all about her when I started this ill-advised matchmaking. Someday I'll learn to think first and talk later.

"This has nothing to do with Denise," Pat said. "This is completely apart from our relationship."

She hurried to the back of the boat.

Suzette left Madame Fouchet and came over to our group. She looked stunning. How could she look so cool and beautifully put together on such a scorching day, I wondered.

"What did she ask you, Janice?" Suzette said, pronouncing my name "Janeese," which I liked. It sounded a lot classier than Janice.

"Oh, she asked me how well I knew Fouchet, what was Madame doing while he was up on deck, things like that."

"Did she ask you anything about me?" she asked.

"She just wanted to know what Madame was consulting you about," I answered.

"What made you think she was consulting me about anything?" Suzette said, patting her little dog, who was beginning to get restless.

"I assumed she was talking to you about the songs you would sing. Since I don't speak French, I didn't really know, but I saw you showing her some sheet music."

"Yes, that's exactly what we were talking about," Suzette said. "I had just talked to Henri . . . Monsieur Fouchet . . . about 'Padam' and he okayed it."

"Where did you talk to him?" Gini, who had been listening to us, asked.

"Up on deck. But he was too busy getting things ready up there to really talk to me," Suzette said.

"Was there a man from India with him?"

"No, just some of the waiters helping him with the chairs."

"What time was this?" Gini asked.

"Must have been around six," Suzette said. "I'm not good with time, though." Her little dog yipped at her. "Oh, tu as faim?" she cooed. "Excuse me. I've got to feed Pierrot. He has hunger." Pierrot wagged his long silky tail and followed his mistress over to the other side of the boat away from us and the musicians. Suzette put some food in a dish and patted him again.

Gini and I watched her. "Why don't I trust that woman?" Gini asked me in a low voice.

"I have the same feeling," I said. "I don't know why. She hasn't really said anything that I can put my finger on. It's just an instinct."

"Cool it," Gini said, moving her head to indicate that Madame Fouchet, who had been talking to Jean, was coming over to us.

"Bonjour, Hoofers. May I ask what the captain asked you, Janice?"

"Of course. She just asked me about you and Suzette and the waiters," I said. "General questions about where everybody was at the time of the murder."

"Ohh?" Madame said. "She asked you about me? What did you tell her?"

"There wasn't much I . . . ," I began when Pat came toward us, a smile on her face, and told Madame that the captain wanted to talk to her next.

After she left, we surrounded Pat.

"Well," Gini asked, "what happened? Did she come on to you?"

Pat giggled. It is not like Pat to giggle. Ever. "Sort of," she said. "She asked me if we could have lunch together after she finishes here."

"What did you say?" Mary Louise asked.

"I said oui, oui," Pat said, laughing again. It was good seeing her like this. She's usually so intense, so serious. Of the five of us, Pat is the most private. Maybe it's the result of having to hide an important fact about herself for most of her life.

Mary Louise didn't say anything, but we could tell from the expression on her face that she was thinking about Denise.

Pat noticed it too. It was always pretty clear what Mary Louise had on her mind. She could never hide any of her feelings.

"Don't worry, honey," Pat said. "It's just lunch.

Nothing for Denise to be concerned about. I love her, and she knows it. She trusts me. Can't you just let me have an innocent lunch with someone?"

Mary Louise didn't look convinced, but she sort of half-smiled.

The mention of lunch reminded me that I was hungry. My friend, Ken, the keyboard guy, was standing nearby, and he obviously had the same thought. He said to me in a low voice, "Lunch sounds like a good idea. Can I take you to one of my favorite places on the Île Saint-Louis?"

"I'd love it," I said. "Wait a second. I have to ask Tina if we're through here."

When I asked her, she said, "I think the captain is through with us. Wait a second till I find out what's happening tonight."

She tapped Jean on the shoulder. "Do you know if there will be a show tonight?" she asked him.

"Yes," he said. "Believe it or not, the boat is sold out in spite of what happened, so Madeleine decided not to cancel the tour. What do you want to dance to tonight, Tina?"

"We planned on 'Sous le Ciel de Paris'—'Under the Paris Sky,' for our first song," she said. "How is that for you?"

"Perfect," he said. "And just right for this crowd. One of Juliette Gréco's hits."

Tina turned to me. "We're done, Jan. Go have fun."

"All clear, Ken," I said to him. "Be with you in a minute."

Just then, Madame Fouchet came back to the front of the boat to join the rest of us, a worried look on her face. She pulled Suzette to the side to talk to her rapidly in French. Gini edged a little closer to them. I hoped she could hear their conversation. I started to ask her if she could hear them, but she put her finger to her lips for me to be quiet so she could listen.

Madame Fouchet noticed her and moved farther away.

"What did she say, Gini?" I whispered.

"Let's get off this boat, and I'll tell you," she said.

"Ken and I are walking over to the Île Saint-Louis for lunch," I said. "Want to come with us?"

"I'd love it," Gini said. "It's one of my favorite places in Paris. Sort of quaint and elegant. I want to take some photos there. OK with you if I tag along, Ken?"

"Absolutely," he said. "You probably know more about that island than I do."

"Is Le Bon Goût still there?" Gini asked.

"It is," Ken said. "Still really good food. Let's go there."

Since Pat was going to lunch with Captain Chantal, I asked Tina and Mary Louise if they wanted to come with us.

"Thanks," Tina said, "But we're going to Notre-Dame and we'll eat somewhere over there. See you later. Better be back by five o'clock, you guys, because of only one shower."

"Don't worry, boss, Gini said. "We'll be there."

Chapter 6

Another Bite of That Salade Niçoise, S'il Vous Plait

Ken put an arm around each of us, and we ran off the boat and up the small street to the sidewalk along the Seine that led to the Île Saint-Louis. I always love walking along that sidewalk on either side of the river because of all the stalls selling every kind of book you can imagine. Old ones, new ones, children's books, mysteries, romances. If you had enough patience, you could find anything you wanted.

By the time we got to the Île Saint-Louis, we were hot and thirsty. Ken led us down the narrow little streets, past elegant town houses, little shops selling flowers, a church, some bakeries, and an ice cream place that Gini said people came from all over Paris to visit, and finally we arrived at Le Bon Goût, a dark, cool, intimate café.

Inside, the room was small and cozy, with net curtains at the windows, white tablecloths, thick napkins standing upright in the wineglasses, a bar in the back, and a large, old-fashioned cash register on the shelf.

"This is perfect," I said as we sat down at a table and ordered cold white chardonnays for Gini and me and a beer for Ken.

"This brings back so many memories," Gini said. "I must have come here a hundred times to photograph this island. Especially when all the flowers were in bloom in the spring. I always wanted to live on this island, but it's so expensive."

"You guys must make a lot of money dancing," Ken said. "Why don't you buy an apartment here and come back when you're not tapping?"

Gini and I looked at each other and exploded into laughter. "You've got to be kidding," Gini said. "We get just enough for our costumes and the meals we eat when we're in Paris or some other exotic place. We love it, but we'll never get rich this way."

"You always look great," Ken, our affable, good-natured ex-pat, said. "I assumed you earned a lot of money."

"If we ever figure out how to do that, we'll let

you know," Gini said, breaking off a piece of the baguette on her butter plate.

"What about you, Ken?" I asked. "Do you get paid a lot on the Bateau Mouche?"

"Wish I did," he said. "It's OK, but not enough to live on the Île Saint-Louis. I think it's the best place to live in Paris."

The waiter took our orders—a croque monsieur for Gini, a salade Niçoise for me, and a hamburger and French fries for Ken.

"How can you order a hamburger in Paris?" I asked him.

"Sometimes I just need something really American," he said, leaning over to kiss my cheek. "Like you."

Nice. I liked this guy. "Liked" is the operative word here.

Gini was her usual fidgety self, looking around to find something to photograph. She's always afraid she'll miss something, our Gini. I'm always afraid I'll find too much. I guess you could say we complement each other. That's why we're such good friends.

"Relax, Gini," I said. "Tell me what you heard Madame Fouchet telling Suzette in French back there on the bateau."

She took a sip of the cold, deliciously dry wine and said, "I couldn't hear everything, but the main thing was that she was urging Suzette not to leave the Bateau Mouche to go to New York to sing in Anderson's nightclub. She was really upset.

That woman is consumed by keeping that boat going, making money for her, and she was very anxious for Suzette to stay. She's their biggest draw, after all. I heard her say she would double her salary if she stayed in Paris and didn't go to New York."

"What did Suzette say to that?" Ken asked.

"She didn't say much," Gini said, "but it sounded to me like she was determined to go with Anderson. She wants to be in New York. Tell me about Suzette, Ken. What's she like, really? Did she fool around with Fouchet or Claude or both of them? I'm really confused about her."

"Everyone is confused about Suzette," Ken said. "She doesn't let anyone know what she's thinking or feeling. I feel sorry for Claude because he does love her and she treats him like dirt. One minute she's all lovey-dovey and sweet, the next minute she's sleeping with Henri."

"How come Madame Fouchet doesn't hate her?" I asked. "She must know about Suzette and her husband."

"Well, since Madeleine is fooling around with Jean, she doesn't really care what her husband did with Suzette," Ken said. "It made it easier for her to be alone with Jean. Madame and Suzette are sort of friends. Or at least I see them talking together a lot. I don't really know the inside story about all this. They like my music, but they don't confide in me much—I suppose because I'm an American."

"I probably shouldn't say this," Gini said, as if that ever stopped her, "but Madame—Madeleine—whatever her name is—sure doesn't seem to be devastated or even a little bit sorry that her husband is dead. I'm beginning to think she might have killed him. What do you think?"

Ken ordered another beer from the waiter when he brought our lunches. Gini and I asked for more wine. I took one bite of my salade Niçoise with anchovies, green beans, potatoes, plum tomatoes, and black olives and closed my eyes in ecstasy.

"I have to find out how to do this," I said. "Whatever this dressing is, it's heaven."

"Ask the waiter before we leave," Ken said. "He'll tell you. They're really nice here. Especially if you ask in French, Gini."

"Remind me, Jan," Gini said. "I'll ask him. I'd also love to get the recipe for this croque monsieur." She stuffed another forkful in her mouth. "The French do something to this simple grilled cheese that makes it incredible. But to get back to our conversation, Ken, do you think Madame killed her husband?"

"She certainly acted guilty—or coldhearted, at least," he said. "More worried about publicity than about Henri's murder. But the thing is, she was in the dining room supervising the staff and then in the front of the boat with us, going over the music. I never saw her leave that part of the bateau during the time somebody shot him."

"Maybe she hired somebody to kill him," Gini said.

"That occurred to me, too," Ken said. "Like that Indian guy. Nobody seems to know who he was or what he was talking to Henri about. When Suzette went up on deck to talk to him she said there was nobody with him."

"I was talking to Alan Anderson this morning at the Jardin du Luxembourg," I said. "He said it was probably somebody in the Mafia who killed him because he wouldn't pay for protection."

"Sounds like an old movie made in the thirties," Ken said. We'll just have to leave it up to that amazing Captain Chantal to solve it." He grinned. "I wouldn't mind getting to know her better."

"Forget it, love," I said. "She butters her toast on the other side."

Ken looked stunned. "How do you know that?"

"She asked me out," I said, cracking up at the expression on his face.

"Are you going?" he asked.

"No, I'm stuck with liking guys," I said. "But Pat is having lunch with her right now. Can't wait to find out what happened."

Ken took my hand and kissed it. "Could you be stuck liking me?"

"Of course, chéri," I said, taking my hand back. "I'll follow you anywhere."

"I'll take you everywhere," he said. "Where do you want to go after this?"

"I know you'll think this is silly," I said, "but I'd love to ride on a carousel. It's sort of a hobby of mine—to ride on a merry-go-round in every new place we go."

"That's not silly," he said. "I'm crazy about carousels. I'll take you to the one in the Tuileries. Want to come, Gini?"

"Sure," she said. "I want a picture of you and Jan riding around on wooden horses. But we told Tina and Mary Louise we'd meet them at Notre-Dame. Let's take the Pont Saint-Louis— that's a bridge, Jan—over to the Île de la Cité, check out Notre-Dame, find our friends, and then walk over to the Tuileries from there. Does that sound like a plan?"

Ken flashed a look of disappointment at me, because I think he wanted to be alone with me. But in his usual good-natured way, he said, "What do you say, Jan? Church before fun?"

I had totally forgotten about Notre-Dame. "Of course," I said. "We can't leave Paris without seeing Notre-Dame."

Gini asked the waiter for the recipe for the salade Niçoise and the croque monsieur. He returned in a few minutes with the recipes neatly typed out in English. "People ask him all the time," she said, and handed them to me.

We took a last sip of wine, paid our bill, and found another narrow, charming street that led to the bridge that crossed over to the neighboring Île de la Cité and Notre-Dame.

RECIPES FOR SALADE NIÇOISE AND CROQUE MONSIEUR

Salade Niçoise
Serves four hungry people or six not-so-hungry people.

Sauce Vinaigrette (one cup)
4 tsps. mustard
Salt and pepper
1 tsp. chopped garlic
8 tsps. red wine vinegar
1 cup corn oil
2 tsps. chopped fresh rosemary

Potato Salad
4 medium-size potatoes steamed whole, with skin on, until tender (not too soft; about 20 minutes)
1½ tbsps. shallots
Salt and pepper
3 tbsps. white wine
3 tbsps. water

Rest of the Salade
2-ounce can flat anchovies in olive oil
3 tbsps. capers
1 large head Boston lettuce
10 plum tomatoes, halved
½ lb. green beans blanched and chilled (I won't tell if you use frozen beans)

3 hard-boiled eggs, peeled and halved
¾ cup pitted Kalamata olives
1 large can tuna
3 tbsps. chopped parsley

To make the sauce vinaigrette
1. Mix the mustard, salt and pepper, garlic, and vinegar together.
2. Whisk in the oil until you have a thickened sauce.
3. Add the rosemary.

To make the potato salad
1. Cut the potatoes into ½-inch slices.
2. Toss the potatoes with the shallots.
3. Add about ¼ tsp. salt and several grinds of pepper.
4. Add wine and water and toss the potatoes some more.
5. Add about ¼ cup of the vinaigrette sauce and toss. Chill.

Arranging the salad
1. Toss the lettuce with the sauce vinaigrette and arrange the leaves around the outside of a large oval platter.
2. Put the potatoes in a circle in the center.
3. Place the tuna in the middle of the potatoes and sprinkle some dressing on the tuna.
4. Place the tomatoes around the potatoes;

sprinkle the vinaigrette on them and add a little salt.

5. Add dressing and salt and pepper to the green beans, toss them, and arrange them in groups of five or six around the platter, next to the tomatoes.

6. Place the halved eggs where they look the prettiest on the platter, and decorate them with an anchovy and a couple of capers on top.

7. Add the black olives around the potatoes.

8. Toss some parsley on top of the tuna, and you have a beautiful salad to serve.

Croque Monsieur

4 tbsps. canola oil
4 slices white bread
4 slices Gruyère or Swiss cheese
2 slices honey-cured ham

1. Preheat oven to 400 degrees.
2. Oil a cookie sheet.
3. Dip one side of each slice of bread in the canola oil.
4. Put one slice of cheese on the oiled side of all four slices of bread.
5. Place a slice of ham on two of the slices of cheese.
6. Make two sandwiches that each have a slice of cheese on the top, covered by a slice of ham, covered by the other slice of cheese.
7. Dunk both sides of the sandwich in the oil, put them on the cookie sheet, and cook in the oven for ten minutes.

If you want to make a Croque Madame, substitute chicken for the ham.

I know this sounds like a plain old grilled cheese sandwich, but it's really much better. Give it a try.

Janice's Fashion Tip: Flip-flops or sneakers: non. Sandals: mais oui!

Chapter 7

Only 387 Steps to the Top

"I could spend my life photographing this cathedral," Gini said. She already had her camera out and was clicking away.

When I first saw this Gothic cathedral with Derek on our honeymoon, I remember being overwhelmed by the sheer size of it, the intricate carving of saints on the huge door that led into the church, the gargoyles peering out from the roof. Inside there were tour groups and tourists taking pictures of the gigantic, awesome rose window, the sunlight shining through it to cast its brilliant colors on the dark wood of the pews and statues. At the front of this vast interior,

Christ on the cross dominated the altar, with statues of Louis XIII and Louis IV kneeling before him.

Ken and I left Gini shooting away, moved around the hordes of tourists in the plaza outside the church, and opened the heavy door to enter the cathedral. There were so many people inside I wondered how we would ever find Tina and Mary Louise. I was soon caught up again in the feeling that God Himself was in that edifice. In spite of all the people listening to tour guides, or walking slowly past the smaller altars on the side adorned with statues of saints, the sounds of voices could hardly be heard because of the glorious organ music filling the vast interior.

I sat down in one of the pews and bowed my head. I wanted to say thank you for this day, for my life, for my friends, and for my daughter. It was as if some hand had guided me there.

Ken sat down next to me, and when he saw that my eyes were closed, he bowed his head too. He was the kind of person who followed along with whatever was happening at the moment. Whatever everybody else was doing. Like a little puppy. I couldn't help but like him, but he wasn't the kind of man I fell in love with.

I'm drawn to men who are leaders, forceful and strong, with definite ideas about what will happen next. This does not often lead to harmonious relationships, but men like Ken bore

me, because they're too nice. As many thera-
pists, including my friend Pat, have often told
me, I'm still looking for my exciting but extremely unreliable father. Unfortunately, I keep
finding him. I'd be a lot better off if I could set-
tle down with someone less exciting and more
dependable—read duller.

Three marriages and three divorces later, I
still look for intellectually challenging partners.
After our adventure in Spain on the luxury train,
I was sure Tom Carson, an actor I've known for
years, was right for me, and we've been seeing
each other in New York. He's a good combination of interesting and reliable. He divorced his
wife, who was with him on that trip, and wants
me to marry him. I go back and forth. A fourth
marriage seems way too risky. I realized I hadn't
called him since I left New York and promised
myself I would get in touch with him when I had
the chance.

After a few minutes of thanking God, I felt
Ken's eyes on me.

"You're so beautiful," he said.

"You're nice," I said, and only I knew it wasn't
a compliment.

I stood up and looked around. "We should find
Tina and Mary Louise," I said. "Let's go back outside and see if they turn up."

The plaza was even more crowded with tourists.
At first, I couldn't find Gini, but her red hair al-

ways attracts attention. I caught sight of her talking to our missing Hoofers across the way.

I ran over to them, Ken close behind.

"Where have you been?" I asked them. "I didn't see you inside the church."

"We climbed up the three hundred and eighty-seven steps on the outside of Notre-Dame to the top, where you can see the gargoyles up close and all of Paris below," Tina said, her face still flushed from the effort on such a warm day in July. "It was amazing, Jan. You should do it."

"Three hundred and eighty-seven steps," I said. "Oh, Tina, I don't think so. The carousel in the Tuileries is more my style. Ken and I are going over there now. Want to come?"

"I don't think I'll walk anywhere except over to that café for a cold drink," she said. "Don't forget, Jan. Be back at the apartment by five-thirty."

She and Mary Louise headed for the café.

"Gini, you still want to come to the carousel with us?" I asked.

"Think I'll change my mind, Jan," she said. "The view from the top of the cathedral is the best one in Paris. I'm taking the three hundred and eighty-seven steps to the top." She shaded her eyes and looked up at the spires of the church. "I'll catch up with you later." I knew she would be up there forever taking pictures of her city.

"See you," I said. "Have fun, Gini. Come on, Ken, let's head for the Tuileries."

Ken and I pushed our way through the crowded plaza and took the Pont d'Arcole over to the right bank. We moseyed along, enjoying the sound of people speaking French all around us, the stalls selling prints of Paris's monuments and boulevards, the sightseeing boats motoring by on the Seine below us, the tourists peering at maps planning their next foray into this always fascinating, never disappointing City of Light.

"There's the Louvre," Ken said, pointing to the right to the glass pyramid that served as the entrance to the massive museum. "The Tuileries are just behind it."

"I wish we had time for the Louvre," I said. "Two of my favorite paintings are there. Vermeer's *The Lacemaker* and his *The Astronomer*."

"You like Vermeer?"

"I adore him," I said. "I love the way he uses light and shadow, the way he paints fur and velvet and lace. You can practically feel them when you look at his paintings. He painted only thirty-five paintings in his whole life, and I want to see every one of them before I'm through. That's on my bucket list."

"How many have you seen so far?" Ken asked.

"Not many. A couple in the Metropolitan Museum, one at the National Gallery in Washington. Three in the Frick Collection in New York.

My favorite there is *Mistress and Maid*—I have a print of it in my bedroom at home. There's a whole story in that painting. The maid is handing her mistress—she's dressed in yellow velvet with ermine trim, and there are pearls winding through her chignon—a note from her lover, the music teacher. I've made up a whole thing about their love affair and . . ."

I stopped. Not everyone is as thrilled as I am about Vermeer's paintings and the stories they hint at. I could tell that Ken's attention was wandering, so I stopped.

"I once saw *Girl with a Pearl Earring*," he said. "It was on tour, and I think I saw it at the Louvre. Not sure. Don't worry, Jan. I'll take you to see your Vermeers before you leave Paris. I promise. Oh, look, we're at the Tuileries. Let's go find the carousel."

I followed Ken past the wide basin where children were sailing boats, past the flowers blooming on all sides of us, past the modern sculptures on exhibit next to the ancient ones of heroes slaying monsters and gods and goddesses, past people reading or dozing in the chairs around the basin. Then, there it was—the merry-go-round, circling, full of children, some laughing, some not so sure they liked it, while their mothers and nannies either stood beside them or waved to them from the side.

"Are you coming on with me?" I asked Ken.

"Of course I am," he said. "Think I'd let you have all the fun?"

We bought tickets and climbed onto outside horses. As the accordion music played "Padam, Padam, Padam," we circled round and round, the only adults on the horses.

I was reveling in the feeling of being a child again. It was my favorite way to stop time. As long as I was riding this painted horse, time was suspended. I was eight years old again, away from my quarreling parents, away from school, away from other children who didn't understand me or my love of the theater, my wanting to be a part of it someday. No responsibility for raising a child or keeping a husband happy here on this joyful carousel. I turned and smiled at Ken riding the horse in back of me. I could see that he was caught up in this moment of long ago as much as I was. He was still a child at heart too.

He smiled back. "Yo, Jan!" he shouted. "Hang on."

When the carousel slowed down and stopped, he came to help me off my horse and kissed my forehead when we were back on the ground again.

"Nice, huh?" he said. He was like a big, old, loved teddy bear. I couldn't resist the urge to hug him.

"Nothing better," I said. "Now where do we go?"

"Let's go over to the Place de la Concorde,"

he said. "It's just across from the Tuileries. You can see the fountain and the obelisk from here."

"Come on," I said, taking his hand and heading for the exit gates from the Jardin des Tuileries, pulling him to the fountain that marked one end of the Champs Élysées. I took a couple of pictures of Ken with my iPhone, and he took some of me.

"What time is it getting to be?" I asked reluctantly. I didn't want to leave.

"It's almost five," he said. "We'd better get back. "Metro or walk?"

"Definitely walk," I said. "Is it far?"

"We can make it in half an hour," he said. "We take the Concorde bridge and walk down Boulevard Raspail to your apartment on Montparnasse."

It was hard not to stop in the shops along the way. There was an open-air market selling the most beautiful fruits and vegetables, the freshest meats, the most gorgeous flowers. Ken had to drag me away from them because he knew I had to be back by five-thirty.

He was a little off in his estimate of half an hour. My forays into the market didn't help, but at quarter of six I was back at our apartment.

"See you soon," I said. "Thanks, Ken. You're a great guide."

He leaned over and kissed my cheek. "And you're a great everything," he said. "À bientôt."

I found my Hoofers in various stages of dressing for our performance that night. Clothes were thrown everywhere, and there were sounds of tap shoes as one of my fellow dancers moved around the main room.

"Oh, Jan, there you are," Tina said. "Glad you're back. Everyone else has showered. It's all yours."

I shed my clothes and jumped into the narrow shower, reveling in the hot water that washed away the dust of the day. It felt great.

I wrapped myself in a thick towel and ran into the bedroom, where Gini was just fastening the buckles on her tap shoes. She looked sensational in the white, tight-fitting, all-lace dress like the ones we all were wearing that night. She had on onyx and silver art deco earrings that were perfect with the dress.

"Sorry I didn't get to the carousel this afternoon, Jan," she said to me. "It took me a while to climb to the top of Notre-Dame, and when I finally got there I couldn't stop taking pictures. It was just spectacular. You should go up there before we leave Paris."

I knew I never would, but I made some vague sounds and squeezed into my own lace dress, which seemed to fit better than when I'd bought it. I must have lost weight with all the walking we were doing in Paris. What a great way to lose some pounds!

"Any more news about Monsieur Fouchet?" I asked her.

"I haven't heard anything," she said. "Maybe when we get to the bateau, we'll find out more."

Tina poked her nose in the door. "You both look incredible," she said.

"You too, Tina," Gini said. "Are we still dancing to 'Sous le Ciel de Paris'?"

"Oui," she said. "A tribute to Yves Montand and Edith Piaf."

"Think there will be many people tonight?" I asked. "I mean, the murder has been in all the papers."

"Alan told me they're fully booked," Tina said. "Go figure."

"Maybe they think the body is still up on the top deck," Gini said, "and they'll get to see it."

"Who knows?" Tina said. "I know nothing about the rest of show business. That's your specialty, Jan."

"If I ever figure out why people like some kind of entertainment, or some kind of music, or some kind of book better than others, I'll let you know. Meanwhile, let's keep dancing."

"The car will be here in twenty minutes, guys," she said. "Finish dressing and we'll go downstairs to wait for it."

I pulled my hair back into a chignon, and Gini wove some fake pearls through it for me—a touch of Vermeer I couldn't resist. Earrings, makeup, tap shoes, and I was ready.

Pat and Mary Louise were stunning in lace. In fact, we all looked like we were born to dance under the Paris sky, as the song says. Where lovers kiss, music enchants, and rainbows drive the clouds away.

Oh yeah, and someone gets murdered.

Janice's Fashion Tip: Splurge on a lightweight cashmere sweater for those cool summer nights.

Chapter 8

Moonlight in Paris

When the five of us stepped aboard that boat in our skinny little lace dresses, our faces made up within an inch of their lives to look as if they were au naturel, our black-stockinged legs with sequins up the back completing the whole picture of gorgeous Happy Hoofers at their sexiest, every man in the band stood up and cheered. Even Yves managed a feeble "Ooh la la."

The three women—Madame Fouchet, Suzette, and Captain Chantal—standing near them were more restrained.

"Bonjour, les Hookers," Madame Fouchet said. "Très chic."

"Are we doing 'Sous le Ciel'?" Suzette asked.

"Yes," Tina said. "Ça va?"

"Ça va," Suzette said. "I love that song." She was stunning, her very sexiest, in a long, white silk dress, slit up the middle to show off her legs.

"I look forward to hearing you," Captain Chantal said, unable to take her eyes off Pat. The captain was wearing a black lace mini that showed off a body her uniform hid almost entirely during the day.

"Anything new about Monsieur Fouchet?" Tina asked the captain.

"The investigation is still underway," she said stiffly. "There are many people to interrogate."

"She's a bundle of laughs," Gini muttered to us.

"She's dealing with a murder, Gini," Pat snapped at her. "What do you expect her to do—offer us a drink?"

Gini started to say something but stopped herself when she saw Pat's face. It was obvious that she was genuinely offended by Gini's remark. I realized I hadn't asked Pat about her lunch with the police captain the day before. Must have been a lot more interesting than I thought.

As seven o'clock approached, people began to crowd onto the bateau, and by seven-thirty every seat was filled. There was an air of excitement, an expectation that this would be more than a tour of Paris's buildings and monuments.

After the first course of foie gras and a glass of

wine, Jean appeared, bowed to the audience and in English said, "Good evening, ladies and gentlemen. We are pleased to have with us this evening America's Happy Hoofers, five beautiful women who will show you how much they love Paris in their dance. Mademoiselle Suzette Millet will sing 'Sous le Ciel de Paris'—'Under the Paris Sky'."

We joined arms and stepped forward to smile at the people waiting to see us perform. The band started the first notes of "Sous le Ciel de Paris." We moved around the stage, first slowly grapevining, then dancing the time step faster and faster, then shuffle-stepping single file down the aisle between the tables, while Suzette sang of a young man in love, a sailor's accordion, a philosopher and a musician, of Notre-Dame, beggars sleeping under the bridges over the Seine, all beneath the Parisian sky. It was a love song to this City of Light. We felt it deep inside as we danced. You could hear it in Suzette's voice. It was as if for those few minutes we were French. We turned and shuffle-stepped back to the stage, bowing as the crowd applauded and cheered our dancing and Suzette's singing.

"And now, mesdames and messieurs," Jean said. "Please join us on the top deck, where you will see Paris at her very best, her monuments illuminated, the sky alight with stars, the very air caressing you as our Bateau Mouche moves along the Seine."

The passengers took a last bite of their main course and left their tables to climb the steps to the upper deck. I held my breath, half-expecting to hear a scream as the first person stepped outside. But it was all right. No screams.

"Come on, Jan. Let me show you Paris at night," Ken said as he took my hand and led me to the stairway. We joined the crowd working its way up the narrow steps. When we got to the top, I breathed in the fresh night air and said, "Ohhhhhhh." I couldn't help it. The moon was full, and there, shining against the starlit sky, were the towers of Notre-Dame, the majestic, awe-inspiring, fourteenth- century Gothic cathedral we had seen that afternoon. But how different to see it at night, without people swarming around it, as if God held it in the palm of His hand. Tears came to my eyes, the way they always do when I see or hear or feel something so powerfully beautiful there are no words to describe it.

"Are you crying?" Ken asked, his voice soft, concerned.

I nodded. "I love this city," I said.

"It *is* wonderful, isn't it?" Mary Louise said, joining us, giving me a quick hug when she saw the tears on my cheek. "I know just how you feel, Jan. It takes your breath away. I don't know how anyone can deny that God exists when they're in this city."

Of all the Hoofers, Mary Louise is the one who could best understand the depth of my feeling. She is the only one in our group who was brought up a Catholic. Her religion is so deeply ingrained in her that she has never questioned her faith. She had her doubts about some of the practices of the Church, but never her belief in God. Whatever happened in her life, she believed it was God's will, and she accepted it. Mary Louise was the embodiment of love. She could not look at another human being in trouble and not try to help. She was the soul of our group of dancers, just as Tina was our heart, Gini our creativity, and Pat our wisdom. I, perhaps, was our adventurer.

Another flash of white and Gini was beside us with her camera. "Can you believe this?" she said, not looking at us, just scanning the shore to get the best angle. She wouldn't have noticed if my tears had flooded the deck and she was standing ankle-deep in them. I love Gini, but she's not exactly the most empathetic person in the world. We're all different, and to tell the truth, that's what I treasure the most about us.

The ship moved along slowly, and a large building on the left side of the boat loomed up, illuminated to stand out from the other sights along the shore.

"Ken, what's that?" I asked.

"It's the Musée d'Orsay," he said. "An art museum. I think I like it better than the Louvre. They have Impressionists. My favorites."

"Mine too," Gini said, putting down her camera briefly. "We have to go there tomorrow," she said to me and Mary Louise. She hadn't really looked at me until that moment.

"Jan," she said, real concern on her face. "Are you all right? Are you crying? What's wrong?"

"I'm fine, Gini." I said, smiling at her. "Just kind of carried away by this city."

"I know," she said. "I'd give anything to live here again."

"Why don't you?" Ken asked. "There's an empty apartment in my building. In fact, why don't all you Hoofers move here?" He looked over at me and brushed away the tear on my cheek. "OK, Jan?"

I nodded and smiled at him.

"Tempting," Gini said. "But there's too much at home that I don't want to leave."

"His name is Alex," Tina said, popping up beside us. "Right, Gini? Have you called him since we've been here?"

"Sure. We talk all the time," she said. "He loves Paris as much as I do."

"I get it," Ken said. "But if you ever change your mind . . ."

"Don't you miss America?" I asked him.

"Sometimes," he said. "Not often. I'm free here to do what I want."

"And what is that exactly?" I asked.

"Play music," he said. "That's all I've ever wanted to do."

"Can't you do that at home?" Mary Louise asked.

"Not like here. At home there are always people pushing me to make more money, get married, be respectable. Here nobody cares what I do as long as I show up on time and play music."

We were all silent. For my part, I wanted someone to care about what I did. Maybe Tom Carson was that someone. I still wasn't sure.

Another monument rose up on the shoreline, its huge dome golden in the dark.

"That's Les Invalides," Gini said. "Napoleon is buried there. They have concerts. We have to go." She turned her camera toward the building and snapped away.

As the bateau approached the Eiffel Tower, not just illuminated but flashing its own lights on and off, showy and spectacular, Pat and Captain Chantal came up on deck, talking to each other so intently, they didn't notice us standing there at first. They made a great-looking couple—Pat in white lace, the captain in black lace. I wondered how far things had progressed with them. They certainly seemed to be more than just friends.

"Hey, Hoofers," Pat said when she saw us all together. "Is this the best or what?"

"You're just coming on deck now?" Gini asked. "You missed the best part."

Pat exchanged glances with Captain Chantal,

and we realized she hadn't missed anything at all.

"Don't worry, Gini," she said. "Geneviève pointed out the batiments and told me all about them as we passed. You can see them downstairs through the windows too."

I could not wait to get Pat alone to find out what was going on with her and the police captain.

The boat passed the Palais de Chaillot, turned around, and pulled up to the dock near the Pont d' l'Alma. People went down the stairs, back to their tables, where chocolate mousse and coffee were waiting for them. When they finished, they left the boat, smiling, talking softly, obviously pleased with their evening.

I was too revved up to leave the deck and go back to the apartment. I wanted something more. Something exciting. For once I felt beautiful. Paris does that to you.

"You're lovely," a man's voice said. I turned around to see Alan Anderson behind me. He looked dark and intriguing. He was wearing a charcoal gray, expertly tailored suit, a white shirt, and a blue-and-red-striped tie. His brown hair was cut perfectly, the way they do in Paris, framing a tanned face that reminded me of the French actor Alain Delon.

He held out his hand. "Come," he said. "I'll show you my Paris at night."

I was mesmerized. I couldn't take my eyes off him. I would have followed him straight into the gates of hell if he'd led me there. I took his hand.

"Jan?" Tina said.

"I'll be back later, Tina," I said. "Don't wait up."

Alan took me down the stairs and off the boat.

"Where are we going?" I asked.

"You'll see," he said.

Chapter 9

Another Glass of Veuve Clicquot?

A black limo was waiting for Alan on the pier. He opened the door for me, and I climbed into the car. A man in uniform at the wheel turned briefly to nod at me. "Bonsoir, mademoiselle," he said. I stammered out my own version of "good evening." Alan sat down beside me, put his arms around me, and kissed me as if I belonged to him. I didn't want him to stop—ever. Few men have kissed me as expertly, as masterfully as he did.

"You are so beautiful, Janice," he said. "I'm taking you to my private club off Saint-Germain. We'll drink champagne, listen to music from long ago, and get to know each other."

I would have gone anywhere, done anything this man asked me.

The car glided smoothly through the streets of the Left Bank until we arrived at a building away from the noise of nearby cafés. The chauffeur opened the door for me, and Alan rang the bell. A window opened in the door, and a dark-faced man immediately opened it for us. He was wearing a Nehru-type jacket with a white flower pinned to his shoulder, and one gold earring gleamed against his brown skin.

"Ah, Monsieur Anderson," he said, with a slight Indian accent. "Bienvenue."

"Bonsoir, Ahmet," Alan said. "My regular table, please."

Ahmet led us into the club, where each table was nestled into a nook away from the other customers. Only two other tables were occupied. There was a dance floor in the middle. The lighting was dim, the music soft, soothing, from another era. Tony Bennett's voice was singing "I Do Not Know a Day I Did Not Love You" as we sat down on a soft, black-leather banquette in one corner of the room.

"Champagne, please, Ahmet," Alan said. "Veuve Clicquot. Brut." He took my hand and kissed it. "I could look at you forever." He reached behind me and loosened the pins in my chignon. My hair fell down around my shoulders. He handed me the pearls that had wound around it. "You should have diamonds in your hair."

I pulled away from him. Enchanted as I was by this fascinating man, I realized I knew nothing about him. Why wasn't he with Suzette instead of me? Wasn't he trying to persuade her to go to New York and appear in his nightclub? Was he having an affair with her?

"Alan," I said, "tell me more about your night-club in New York. What's it like? Where is it? I want to go there when I get back."

"It's in the West Village," he said, "on a little street hidden away from the main streets. We play a lot of music from other countries, especially France. It's intimate, romantic, and we're full every night."

"So that's why you want Suzette to go there?" I said.

His face closed up. He looked away from me. "Yes, she would be perfect at my club."

"What's it called?" I asked.

"Le Bateau Mouche," he said.

"Can't wait to go there," I said. "I heard there were problems with Suzette leaving the boat here."

"Yes. Henri tried to keep her from leaving. He knows people in the government, and he tried to get them to confiscate her passport. Now that is no longer a problem." He lit a cigarette and greeted Ahmet, who appeared with a bottle of champagne and two glasses.

"Ah, bon," he said.

When Ahmet filled a glass for each of us, Alan raised his in a toast to me. "To your beauty," he said.

"To your choice of clubs," I said, taking a sip of the excellent champagne.

"They call them boîtes here," he said.

"I thought Madame Fouchet was against your taking Suzette away too," I said. "I mean, she's so perfect for the bateau."

"Oh, my lovely Janice, let's not get into all that. It will be resolved. Do not worry." He stubbed out the cigarette and poured himself another glass of champagne.

It was clear that we weren't going to talk about anything too serious tonight, so I shut up about Suzette and New York and Madame Fouchet. But I had a lot of questions. I wanted to ask him if he still thought it was someone in the Mafia who had killed Fouchet. It was obvious that he didn't want to discuss it.

Alan stood up and reached for my hand. "Come dance with me," he said.

He took me in his arms on the dance floor as Edith Piaf's voice embraced us with "Les Feuilles Mortes," one of my favorite songs in the world. "Autumn Leaves." I closed my eyes. Alan danced with me as if he were making love to me. His body was close against mine, and he was an excellent dancer, so we moved together as if we were one person. Not many men can dance like that. At least not American men. I hummed along as we danced, and he whispered in my ear, "I have a room upstairs in this club," he said. "Will you come there with me?"

I was under no illusion that this room was anything but a bedroom. Did I want to go? You bet. Should I go? Probably not. What a shame. He was probably really good at what we would be doing up there.

"I need more time, Alan," I said. "Not tonight."

The song ended. He kept holding me in his arms and kissed me. "Are you sure?"

"I'm afraid so," I said. "I'd better be getting back to the apartment. This was wonderful, Alan. Thank you."

"To be continued," he said. We stopped at the table, and I picked up my purse and pearls and we left the club.

He held me close in the limo until we reached my door, kissed me again, and waited until the chauffeur opened the door.

"I adore you, Janice," he said.

"Good night, Alan," I said and went inside to join my friends.

It was after two when I got back to the apartment. When I crept in, Mary Louise was fast asleep on the sofa bed. There was a light under the door of the room I shared with Gini. When I opened it, she was in bed reading her Kindle.

"Well, well," she said when she saw me. "I wasn't sure whether you were coming back tonight or not."

"Neither was I for a while there," I said.

"So what happened with that gorgeous Alan?" she asked.

I told her about Alan and the club and the conversation about Suzette. "He changed the subject fast," I said.

"All he said when you brought up Fouchet was that he wasn't a problem anymore?" Gini asked.

"Yeah, that seemed strange to me too. But he had his mind on other things. He was trying to lure me into a bedroom upstairs."

"What kind of a nightclub is that?" Gini said too loudly.

I shushed her and said, "A private club. Very private. In fact, he owns it."

"How come you didn't go?" she asked.

"I don't know. Something told me to find out more about him."

"Good thinking, Jan." Gini said. Ready as she always was to urge me on to whatever new adventure I had in mind, she was often the voice of reason when it looked like I was going too far. Like the dear and trusted friend she's always been to me.

"Tell me what happened after I left," I said.

"Madame Fouchet invited us, the guys in the band, Captain Chantal, and Suzette to a late supper on the boat. A couple of the waiters stuck around to bring it to us. Mucho wine and fine food."

"Did you talk about Fouchet's murder, or didn't you want to talk about it in front of Madame?" I asked.

"Oddly enough, she brought it up," Gini said. "We were all surprised."

"What did she say?"

"After a little wine, there was a lull in the conversation, and she said to Captain Chantal—or Geneviève, as we call her now—'Have you figured out who killed my husband yet?'

"You could tell Geneviève was startled by the question. She certainly wasn't expecting it, but she's a cool cat. She looked directly at Madame and said, 'We've had a couple of breakthroughs, but I can't talk about it yet.'

"Madame Fouchet—I just can't call her Madeleine—said—listen to this, Jan—she said, 'You must find the murderer soon. I have a feeling I'm next.' "

"She really said that?"

"Can you believe it? Yeah, she really said that."

"What did Chantal say?" I asked.

"She was stunned," Gini said. "But she asked Madame Fouchet why she thought that. Madame said, 'It's nothing I can put my finger on. It's just a feeling.' You know how she always looks so self-assured and above the rest of us? Well, she didn't look that way then. She really seemed scared."

"So what did the captain say then?" I asked.

"She kept trying to pry out of her what was making her feel like that. Finally, Madame lost her cool and said, 'When I got to the boat tonight, the waiter brought me a drink. I hadn't ordered one, but I didn't think much about it. I took a sip and there was definitely something not right about that drink. I threw it out. I'm sure someone is trying to poison me.'"

"You could tell the captain wasn't buying this," Gini said. "She said, 'Did you ask the waiter why he brought you a drink you hadn't ordered?' Madame said, 'By the time I thought of asking him that, he had disappeared. I looked for him, but there was so much to do before the customers arrived, I didn't have time to keep searching. I'm not even sure which waiter it was. But I'm sure someone is trying to kill me.' Jan, she was practically hysterical, and that's not like her at all. You know how cool and above-it-all she always is."

"This is really weird," I said. "I thought all along she was the one who killed her husband, but now it looks like she might be a victim. What did the captain say then?"

"She was fantastic," Gini said. "Really good at her job. She did her best to calm Madame down. She said she would assign a police officer to stay with her if she would like, but Madame said no, she didn't want that. So the captain told Madame to call her anytime she had any suspicions that someone was trying to kill her. Even in the middle of the night. To be honest, Jan, none of us really believed her story. A drink tasted funny so she thought she was being poisoned? Come on. How come she didn't have it tested?"

"It does sound a little crazy," I said. "I just hope she doesn't turn up dead. Speaking of dead, I need to sleep. Are you going to read much longer?"

"No, I'm through," she said. "I was really just waiting for you to get home so I could tell you all this. Doesn't it seem to you that we attract murderers and killing and mayhem wherever we go?"

"Nothing happened when we were in Atlantic City," I said.

"What murderer wants to go there?" she asked. I fell asleep laughing.

**Janice's Fashion Tip: Forget your backpack.
Take a cross-body purse to Paris.**

Chapter 10

Water Lilies, Willow Trees, and
What's New

I was still sleeping the next morning when my
phone rang. I had forgotten to turn it off before I went to bed. I fumbled around until I dug
it out of my purse on the floor by the bed.

"Mmpff" was the best I could do.

"Good morning, Jan," a male voice said. I had
no idea who it was.

"Who's this?" I managed to mumble.

"Alan," he said. "Alan Anderson. Remember
me?"

"Oh, Alan, hi," I said, still not fully awake.

"I've been thinking about you a lot. I want to
see you again. Get your gang together," he said.

"I'm taking you to Giverny to Monet's house and gardens. They're spectacular right now, and you can't leave France without seeing them."

"But . . . but . . . ," I stammered. "What time is it?"

"It's eight o'clock," he said. "I know, I know. It's early. But it will take us over an hour to get there—it's sixty miles north of Paris. You can't go back home without seeing the water lilies and the rest of his garden. Get dressed. I'll pick you and your Hoofers up in an hour. Don't worry about breakfast. There'll be coffee, croissants, and hot chocolate in the car."

"Oh, Alan, that's so nice of you, but . . . ," I said.

"No 'buts,' " he said. "I'm not going to let you miss this. Wear something cool. It's supposed to be eighty today. Be downstairs with your gang at nine o'clock." He hung up.

Gini's bed was empty, and I could hear noises from the living room. I still wasn't fully awake. I stumbled out there, rubbing the sleep from my eyes. My friends were munching on muffins and sipping coffee, still in their pajamas.

"Jan, welcome to the world," Gini said. "I thought you'd sleep until noon after your late night with Alan."

"Yeah, tell us about it," Pat said. "Gini said he took you to some private club with a bed upstairs or something. What happened?"

"I'll tell you all about it later," I said. "But right now you have to get dressed."

114

"What's the rush?" Tina said. "I was going to relax and then go to the Pompidou. They've got a whole retrospective of Lichtenstein's paintings—a hundred of them. That museum is fascinating. Lots of standing sculpture you can go inside of. Those escalators with glass arches over them. The whole place is unusual."

"Yeah, and I'm getting my hair cut at this place Suzette told me about," Mary Louise said. "She said there's this young guy there from South Africa who makes you look like a whole new person. A French person. I want to go home looking French. George will go wild."

"If he even notices," Gini said.

"Come on, Gini," Mary Louise said. "He's not that bad. Why don't you come with me? You could use a new look. Alex would notice. He notices everything."

"You can do all that stuff another day," I said, beginning to come alive after a gulp of coffee. "Wait till you hear," I said, my enthusiasm making me speak faster and faster. "Alan is taking us all in his limo to Giverny to see Monet's house and his gardens. He's picking us up at nine. It's supposed to be gorgeous, and he says we can't go home without going there, and he's giving us breakfast in the car and . . ."

"Giverny!" Gini interrupted. "Oh, wow, you guys. It's fantastic. I wanted to go there this week, but there were so many other things to see. I didn't feel like taking the train all the way up there and then the shuttle, but this is incredible, Jan. You must have really impressed him last night."

"If he was that impressed, he would have just asked me to go with him alone," I said. "But he wants all of you to come too. Can't imagine why. You're such a boring group." Mary Louise hit me with her pillow. "So what do you say, gang? I'm going, but it will be much more fun with all of you there too. Say you'll go."

"A limo, you say?" Tina said.

"A limo that comes with croissants and coffee and hot chocolate," I said.

"You're on," Tina, our decision maker, leader, and official voice of the Happy Hoofers said. "Who wants the shower first?"

We managed to shower, dress in the lightest-weight tops and skirts we had, and appear at the door of the building just as Alan's limo pulled up.

He jumped out, smiled broadly when he saw us standing there, and opened the door for us to get in.

"You're all sensational," he said. He kissed my cheek as I climbed into the car.

Amazingly, there was enough room in that limo for all of us to be seated comfortably. As promised, there were little trays with a croissant and a cup for each one of us. Alan introduced us to François, the chauffeur, and then said to him, "To Giverny, François, s'il vous plait."

We crept through rush-hour traffic in Paris

that's ten times worse than New York because of the traffic circles, which slow everybody down. After we hit the open road, we sailed along in Alan's limo, which rode so smoothly we could have been on a magic carpet.

When we arrived at Monet's house an hour later, Alan told François he would call him when it was time to pick us up. He shepherded us into the garden, and the woman in the ticket booth waved us through. "Take good care of these ladies," Alan said. "They're very special."

The woman made it clear she would do anything Alan asked her to. He seems to have that effect on people.

"I have to make a couple of phone calls," he said to us. "I'll find you later and take you to lunch. Enjoy."

It was as if we had stepped into another world. A world of flowers and trees, shrubs and archways, ponds and water lilies. Narrow paths wound in and out of tulips, irises, daffodils, daisies, hollyhocks, and poppies. No mingy little patches of impatiens and asters. Everywhere you looked there were flowering shrubs and overhead roses winding lushly around iron arches. Weeping willows bowed gracefully down to touch the pond, and there was an exquisite little Japanese bridge over it. When we stood on it we were surrounded by lilac trees blessing us with their perfumed flowers. Gini took a picture of all of us on the bridge.

We followed the path through a tunnel under the road to a pond filled with water lilies. Not just the skimpy little white lilies I was used to but three or four nestled together. Some pink, some salmon, some yellow mingling with the white ones. All around us more trees, shrubs, flowers, so thick you felt like you were in a scented forest. I wanted to stay there forever.

Gini hadn't stopped photographing this wonderland from the moment we got there, but she stopped, looked up, focused on us, and said, "You have to see Monet's house. Come on, I'll take you there."

I didn't want to leave this flowery Eden, but I was also dying to see Monet's house. We wound our way back through the tunnel, following the narrow paths to the pink brick house where Claude Monet and his second wife, Alice, lived from 1893 to 1926. One of the founders of the Impressionist school of painting, he has always been one of my favorites because of the light and sunshine pouring through his paintings, many of them done here in his own garden in Giverny.

Whenever there is a Monet exhibit at the Museum of Modern Art in New York, I sit there for hours basking in his sunlight. I was so grateful to Alan for bringing us here. Even if he was doing all this to get me into that bedroom at the club, at the moment it didn't matter. I looked around for him when we got to the house, but he was nowhere in sight.

I didn't really care where Alan was. Once we stepped inside this house it felt like Monet used the same method of bringing light and tranquillity into the rooms that he used in his paintings. Everywhere there were floor-to-ceiling windows filling the rooms with sunlight.

The dining room, especially, was an ode to peace and beauty. The cabinets, a pale yellow, brightened one side of the room. A long table with a white cloth, flowers, and candles filled the center of the room. Windows looking out onto the garden were on the other side. You could easily imagine Monet and his friends Cezanne, Renoir, Pissarro, Sisley, Manet, and other Impressionists sharing this table, talking about art and music, travel and food, wines, everything. It was a room made for friendship and beauty.

Tina tugged at me to come into the kitchen.

"Look at this," she said. "Wouldn't you love to cook in here?"

Actually, there's no place anywhere I'd love to cook in, but I didn't remind her of that. Cooking just isn't one of my favorite things. However, it was a kitchen that even I might want to hang out in. Hung on hooks along one side of this blue, cheerful kitchen was a long line of bright, shiny copper pots of all sizes and shapes. Under them was an incredible coal and wood stove that served up feasts the whole thirty-three years Claude and Alice lived there.

Mary Louise joined us, and I didn't think she would ever leave this room. "I want that stove," she said. "You can't cook anything properly on a gas stove. With this one I could do miracles."

"I'm sure George would love a bunch of coal in the basement," I said. I managed to drag her out of the kitchen into the living room, where paintings by Monet and the other Impressionists hung side by side. One particularly lovely one was of Monet's wife sewing in the garden with her little daughter nearby, both of them in blue dresses, flowers all around them, sunshine and serenity reigning.

There were more paintings by his friends on the narrow stairway leading to the bedrooms upstairs. One small room had exquisite black-and-white Japanese prints on the wall. The furniture was made of light wood, and large windows brightened each room. It was a house that fostered creativity and happiness. No wonder Monet kept painting into his seventies and eighties, even after the death of Alice, whom he adored.

I was admiring a sweet little lavabo with a basin and flowered pitcher in one of the bedrooms when Pat joined me.

"Isn't this house amazing?" I asked her.

"It really is," she said. "I'm getting hungry, though. Could we find Alan and take him up on that lunch offer?"

I wouldn't have cared if I didn't eat all day. I wanted to stay here in this house and these gardens that were the essence of Monet's mission of bringing light and joy into a gloomy world. But Pat lives more in the other side of her brain. The practical, scientific, let's-face-reality side. I have one of those sides to my brain too, but I always find it annoying. I forced myself to put myself in Pat's place. She was hungry. She needed food. I had to find Alan and feed her.

I rounded up the rest of the Hoofers, and we squeezed down the narrow stairway and out the front door. Alan was standing there smiling at us.

"How was it?" he asked. "Are you glad you came?"

We all talked at once as we tried to tell him how much we loved this experience.

"Thank you, Alan," I said. "I wouldn't have missed this for anything."

"You can thank me properly later," he said, hugging me. "Now how about some lunch, ladies? There's a lovely little restaurant right across the street called Nympheas where you feel like you're eating in Monet's garden. And the food is superb. Sound good?"

"Sounds perfect," Pat said. The rest of us agreed, and we walked the short distance to the restaurant.

The host was waiting for us at the entrance. He greeted Alan warmly. Why did I have this feeling that Alan knew everybody everywhere?

"Ah, bonjour, Monsieur Anderson," the host said as we walked through the rose-covered archway into the airy restaurant. "I have a table waiting for you and your très jolies guests out on the patio. Please follow me."

The patio was a cool oasis with a table set up just for us. Thick branches of flowers bloomed around us on all sides. There was a perfect little arrangement of roses and lilies of the valley in a crystal vase at each place setting. The china was Limoges (I peeked), the silver exquisite. There were no other people on the patio. I felt like I was still in Monet's house as one of his honored guests.

"Oh, Alan, this is divine," I said.

"Wait till you taste the food. Josef," he said to the waiter, "a bottle of cabernet and one of chardonnay, please."

"Good choices for our food, sir," the waiter said.

"The cooking here is Norman," Alan said. "Very rich. Very delicious. Hope you're all hungry."

"Rich and delicious sounds exactly what I'm looking for," Pat said, opening the menu, which was in French. "My French is a little rusty. Alan, would you translate?"

"I just tell them to bring me whatever is good," he said. "I think this is a job for Gini. Janice tells me your French is so good even the

French compliment you. They don't do that often."

"I thought it was pretty good," Gini said, "until the other day in a shop I asked for something in French. The owner told me I spoke the language well and was I from Belgium. I lived in France long enough to know that wasn't a compliment. Having a Belgian accent is like having a Jersey accent at home."

"So translate for us, Miss Belgium," Pat said.

"Here we go," Gini said. "Our choice is a salad with smoked salmon and crabmeat, a salad with ham and magret of duck, fillets of pork with Camembert and ceps, or veal cutlet Vallée d'Auge. I think we need our waiter to tell us about these."

Alan motioned to the waiter, who spoke perfect English.

"May I help you?" he asked.

"S'il vous plait," Gini said. "Could you tell us what's in these dishes? What's a magret of duck, for instance? What are ceps? How do you make the veal?"

"These are Norman dishes, mademoiselle, which is probably why you're not familiar with them. Magret of duck is breast of duck, but it's not like the duck breasts you're used to in the United States. These are breasts of the mulard ducks, which are much richer and browner than your duck breasts. They are excellent. The ceps with the pork fillets are a kind of mushroom.

The veal cutlet Vallée d'Auge is also very rich. It's made with calvados, apples, mushrooms, and sour cream. Delicious, but perhaps a bit heavy for a July day. Depends on how hungry you are."

"Everything sounds delicious," Tina said, "but I think the smoked salmon and crabmeat salad with a glass of chardonnay would be just right for today."

We all chose either salads or open sandwiches to go with the wine, and I leaned back in my chair, totally relaxed and happy. *How often can I say that?* I thought. Usually there's something nagging at me. I have to learn that new dance step. Will I be able to work with my daughter, Sandy, on the book about the Gypsy Robe without our fighting with each other? Do I really want to get married again? And if I do, do I want to marry Tom Carson? Should I go back to that club—and possibly that room upstairs—with Alan Anderson? Why do I have reservations about him? He's generous and interesting, and he seems to like me a lot. He's probably a skilled, exciting lover. What's bothering me?

But right now, at this minute, in this lovely restaurant with my best friends all around me, there was nothing to worry about. I was content. I took a deep breath and exhaled contentment.

Tina was sitting next to me, and as usual, she noticed. Tina always notices. "Feeling that good, huh, Jan?" she said in a low voice while the others raved about their lunches.

"I'll take this day home with me to bring out and enjoy when things get tough," I said. "What is it about this place?"

"It's as if Monet hovers over it all, including this restaurant, to bring his vision of happiness to everyone who comes here. It's in the air," Tina said. "Did you notice they have a copy of a menu that features dishes Monet served to his friends? Things like rabbit pie, duck terrine, banana ice cream with lemon madeleines, tarte tatin?"

Alan heard her. "Wait till you taste the tarte tatin," he said. "Then you'll know true happiness. You'll think you're having lunch with Monet."

As if this conversation, all light and joy, needed an antidote, Pat, our practical, face-reality, non-drinking Pat said, "So, Alan, who do you think killed Monsieur Fouchet?"

Gini, who had just taken a sip of her cabarnet, coughed, and a few drops of the red wine fell on the white tablecloth. "Pat!" she said.

"Well, it's on all our minds," she said. "And, Alan, you know these people better than we do. I just thought I'd ask. But if you . . ."

"No, no," Alan said, "that's all right, Pat. I'm sure it was someone from the Mafia—it's the Albanian Mafia in Paris—who tried to get protection money from Henri, and when he wouldn't give it to them, they killed him as a warning to whoever took over from him. Captain Chantal is looking into that."

I felt the tension creeping back into my day of wine and roses. I wished they'd all shut up about the murder. I just wanted another sip of my chardonnay and another bite of my smoked salmon.

Alan stood up. "Excuse me, ladies, my phone is vibrating. I'll be right back." He left the table and went inside the restaurant to take his call.

The mood had changed at the table. Mary Louise tried to bring back the good feeling that existed when we sat down, but it was no use. Even the superb tartes tatin the waiter brought us didn't work.

We ate in silence until Alan came back to the patio. His face was serious.

"We have to get back to the boat," he said. "That was Captain Chantal. She wouldn't tell me what happened, but she said we have to report to her right away."

"Maybe she figured out who killed Fouchet," Gini said.

"I don't think so," Alan said. "I got the feeling that there was something new. Some new development. Anyway, I'm sorry to drag you lovely ladies away from this place of serenity and peace, but the captain made it clear she wants us there as soon as we can get there."

Alan asked the host for our bill. After paying, he led us outside to the limo, where François was waiting. We rode in silence back to Paris.

CANCANS, CROISSANTS, AND CASKETS

How could this be happening to us again? I thought. All we wanted to do was go to wonderful places, dance a little, meet some neat people, eat some delicious food, and return home again, without any involvement with the police and serious crimes. Seems little enough to ask—but not for us, I guess.

Chapter 11

Speeding Through the Louvre

The traffic back to Paris was light, and we were at the boat by three o'clock. Captain Chantal was waiting for us in the main dining room. Suzette, Jean, Claude, Yves, and Ken were seated at a table in back of her. They were all subdued, quiet, except for Yves, who was drumming on the table with a couple of bread sticks. As usual, he didn't seem to be part of this world.

The captain frowned at him, and he stopped.

"Please sit down," she said to us. She was her usual pristine self in her police uniform, starched shirt, polished shoes. Gone was her glamorous image of the night before in black lace. I don't know how she managed to look so cool in all those clothes in this July heat. Sheer willpower, I guessed. She nodded to Pat as we joined the others at their table.

"There has been another murder," she said.

I gasped. Another murder? I thought she was going to tell us that they had found Henri Fouchet's killer.

"Madame Fouchet was shot in the living room of her apartment this morning," Captain Chantal said.

"My God!" Gini said. "I thought she was the one who killed her husband!"

"She still could be his killer," Chantal said. "We don't know who killed him. But it's more likely that somebody wanted both Monsieur and Madame Fouchet out of the way."

Captain Chantal opened her hand. She held a flat gold earring on her palm. It looked vaguely familiar to me, but I couldn't remember where I had seen it. Was Madame wearing it? Or maybe Suzette? Or one of the passengers? Where had I seen it before? It just wouldn't come to me.

"We found this earring near the front door," she said, holding it out so everyone could see it. "We're not sure if it was Madame Fouchet's or if the killer dropped it. Do any of you recognize it?"

No one said anything. Suzette bent down to pat her little shih tzu and fed him a couple of dog cookies.

The guys in the band looked numb. Finally,

Jean spoke, his voice barely audible. "Captain, will this take much longer? I don't feel well."

"Not long, monsieur," Geneviève said. "I know you have been through a terrible experience this morning. I just need to ask you a few questions because you were the one who found her. Did you talk to her before you went to her apartment? Did she say anything that might help us find her killer?"

"All I know is she was terrified that someone wanted to kill her," he said. "You heard her yesterday. She thought there was poison in her drink. I asked her afterward why anyone would want to kill her. She said something vague about the same people who killed her husband would be after her now."

"What people?" the captain asked.

"She said her husband got some threatening phone calls," Jean said. "Something about the Albanian Mafia. I didn't know what she was talking about. I thought the Mafia was Italian."

"Not anymore," the captain said. "One of the most powerful groups of criminals in the world today is the Albanian Mafia. They're very powerful here in Paris. They deal in heroin and other drugs, prostitution, protection, everything."

"She said they wanted her husband to pay them money every month or they would destroy him or the boat or both." Jean said. "He didn't take them seriously. He wouldn't pay them.

They killed him. She was afraid they would kill her next. And they did." He bent over and covered his face with his hands.

"Maybe, maybe not," Captain Chantal said. "We traced the calls that came in to Monsieur Fouchet's cell phone, and all of them could be traced to legitimate sources. However, it's unlikely that they would contact him by phone. They must have visited him in person. Didn't any of you notice him talking to people you didn't recognize?"

"He talks to people every day we've never seen before," Claude said. "It's part of his business. Salespeople. Tourists reserving the boat for weddings and bar mitzvahs. It could be anybody. I'm sure the Mafia doesn't wear a label on their clothes identifying them."

Captain Chantal glared at him. She was clearly skeptical of the whole idea of the Albanian Mafia killing both Monsieur and Madame Fouchet.

"And you, mademoiselle," she said to Suzette. "You were a very—uh—close friend of Monsieur's, n'est-ce pas?"

Suzette was obviously not someone who was thrown easily. "As I told you before," she said, "he was my boss. I was a friend of both Monsieur and Madame Fouchet."

"Then why did you want to leave those good friends to go to New York?" the captain asked.

"It is a great opportunity for me," Suzette said. "I've always wanted to go to New York. Why is that so hard to understand? It has nothing to do with my feelings for Monsieur Fouchet. I liked working for him on this bateau. But it's time for me to move on. To New York."

"Did they try to prevent you from leaving to go with Monsieur Anderson?"

"Oh, you know. They asked me not to go. We were working it out." She leaned over to give Pierrot some more cookies.

"Did they do more than ask you not to go?" the captain asked.

"There was something about my passport, I think."

"What do you mean? Something about your passport?"

"I'm here on a visa from Algeria," Suzette said. "And Monsieur Fouchet said he would prevent it from being renewed if I didn't stay with him. That way I would have no papers to get to New York. But Alan was going to fix all that."

The captain turned to Alan. "Monsieur Anderson, the Fouchets were opposed to you taking Suzette to New York with you to sing in your nightclub there. How did you persuade them to let her go?"

"It wasn't easy, Captain," Alan said. "I tried to make them understand how important this was for Suzette. They were both fond of her. They finally agreed just before they were killed. I'm grateful that I have a place for Suzette to go."

"How fortunate for you that they agreed," Captain Chantal said.

"Very," Alan said. He was calm, composed, almost casual as he answered the police captain's questions. What was it about him that bothered me? I couldn't figure it out. He was the ideal man. Handsome, successful, dynamic, brilliant. Had I become so cynical about men that I couldn't trust any of them anymore? No. Not really. I trusted Tom. I let it go.

"I will be in touch with you soon," the captain said. "Monsieur Anderson, please do not leave the country until this matter is settled."

"I was planning to leave at the end of the week," Alan said. "I have plane reservations. I want Suzette to appear in my club as soon as possible. I've made all the arrangements. People are expecting her in New York."

"I regret that I must ask you to stay," the captain said, "until we have solved this crime."

"Am I accused of anything, Captain?" he asked.

"No," she said, "but I will probably have more questions for you."

"You can't keep me here. I've done nothing wrong." Alan said.

Chantal's faced changed, grew grimmer. "I think I can," she said. As I said before—don't mess with this woman.

Yves starting drumming on the table again until my friend Ken shook his head at him and he stopped.

"You may all leave now," the captain said. "Obviously, there will not be a performance here tonight. Or probably for the rest of the week."

"Does that mean we're free to go back to the United States?" Tina asked.

"If you wish," the captain said. Then she looked at Pat. "But perhaps you would like to explore Paris a little more before you go. There are so many things going on in the summertime. I would be glad to tell you about some of them."

"Maybe," Tina said. "Our apartment is all paid for. We'll think about it."

Captain Chantal took Pat aside, and I heard her say in a low voice, "Perhaps we could meet for tea later, chérie?"

"I'd like that," Pat said. "Where?"

"See you at the George Cinq at five o'clock?"

"I'll be there," Pat said.

The captain left the boat.

"Wow! The George Cinq!" Gini said. "Very posh. Things must be progressing with you and the captain, Pat."

"Oh, Gini, cool it," Pat said. "She's just fascinating to talk to, and I've never been to the George Cinq."

"It's the best," Gini said. "Très expensive and worth every penny. You're supposed to call it the

Four Seasons George Cinq, but nobody does. It will always be just the George Cinq."

"Have you talked to Denise since you've been here?" Mary Louise, our worrier, asked Pat.

Pat smiled at her friend. "Don't worry, hon," she said. "I talk to her every day. I've told her all about the captain, and she's fine with it. She trusts me. She just wishes she were here too."

"I'm glad," Mary Louise said. "I really like Denise." She looked at the time on her phone. "Since we don't have to rush back to the apartment to dress, we've got time to see more of Paris. Who wants to come to the Pompidou museum with me?"

"I'll come," Tina said. "I've never been there, and I hear it's sort of odd and fascinating."

"It is," Mary Louise said. "I can't wait to see the Lichtensteins."

"I'll join you," Gini said. "I don't care about the Lichtensteins—they just look like cartoons to me—but there's a great photography section there with both stills and videos. I missed the Cartier-Bresson exhibit last month, and I want to see who's there now."

"Wait for me," Pat said. "I've never been there either. Jan, how about you? Are you a Lichtenstein fan?"

"Not really," I said. "I think I'll check out the Louvre. There are a couple of Vermeers there I want to see. He's more my style."

"Want company?" Ken asked, putting his arm around me.

"Sure," I said, "I always want your company."

We started down the ramp to leave the boat when Alan pulled me away from the others.

"Have dinner with me at the club tonight, will you, Janice?" he said. "I may not have another opportunity to be with you. I'd like one more dance, one more chance to hold you in my arms. Please say you'll come."

"Oh, Alan, I told Ken I'd go to the Lapin Agile with him."

"You can do that another night," Alan said. "This is my last chance to be with you."

"Go ahead, Jan," Ken, who had overheard, said. "We'll go to Lapin Agile tomorrow night. It will still be there. And I've got you all to myself this afternoon."

Such a sweet man. I kissed him on the cheek. "If you're sure you don't mind," I said.

"Of course not," Ken said.

A last evening with Alan couldn't hurt, could it? Why not?

"I'd love to, Alan," I said. "Pick me up at the apartment at seven."

He kissed my hand. "I'll be there," he said.

"Let's go, Ken," I said. "I have a couple of hours before I have to be back at the apartment. Let's take the Metro."

A short train ride later, we were in the line

waiting to get into the glass pyramid that led to the Louvre. It was fairly short. Almost everybody around us spoke English. American English.

"I'll never forget the first time I came here," Ken said. "A sculptor friend of mine said he would show me the Louvre in half an hour. Half an hour! It's huge. Massive. I asked him how he could do that. 'Watch me,' he said. First he took me to the wide staircase going up to the first floor. You know the one that Audrey Hepburn posed on for Fred Astaire in *Funny Face* wearing all those beautiful clothes?"

"I loved that movie," I said. "In fact, I loved anything Audrey Hepburn ever did."

"Me too," Ken said. "Well, anyway, this guy took me to this staircase and pointed to the *Winged Victory* at the top. We ran up and walked around it— fast. It is incredible. It's a marble statue of Nike, the Greek goddess of victory, supposedly on the prow of a ship greeting a naval fleet just after they won. She has no head or arms, but nobody cares. She represents winning."

"It's the first thing you see when you come into the museum," I said. "Standing there at the head of that impressive stairway, it's awesome."

"Then my sculptor friend said, 'Come on,' and we ran back down the stairs and through a corridor to a small room with the marble statue the *Venus de Milo* in it," Ken continued. "He told me she was the Greek goddess of love and beauty and her name is really Aphrodite. She has no arms either, but her body and face are gorgeous. He pointed out all the things I should appreciate about it. His own sculpture was wood and as far from a classic sculpture as you could get. They were large shapes. I didn't know what any of them were, but I liked to look at them.

"Anyway, after the *Venus de Milo*," Ken said, "he pulled me up the stairs again and into a large room with walls crowded with paintings. There were people everywhere, but mostly in front of one painting set off from the others in a bullet-proof, climate-controlled booth. It was da Vinci's *Mona Lisa*, of course, smiling that smile. It used to hang on the wall next to all the others, but in 2005, he told me, they put it in a protected place, where people can see it but can't touch it. Anyway, I can say I've seen the *Mona Lisa*. I never did understand why it's valued more highly than all the other paintings in the world, but what do I know? My friend said, 'Now you've done the Louvre,' and we left to get a drink somewhere."

I laughed. I thought that was so typical of Ken's attitude toward life. Just do the essentials. Play music, eat, live somewhere beautiful, love whoever is nearby, do the Louvre in half an hour.

"Let's go find my Vermeers," I said.

"They're upstairs," he said.

We headed right for the seventeenth-century Dutch painters on the second floor. First we found Vermeer's *The Astronomer*, a painting of a man reaching up to examine a globe showing the constellations. The light from the window illuminates the globe so that it is the centerpiece of the painting. The astronomer (possibly posed by the scientist Antonie van Leeuwenhoek, the identifying plaque said) is more in the shadows, as are the charts and pictures on the wall to his right. He wears a blue robe, and his hair is shoulder-length. I like this picture, but my favorite is *The Lacemaker*, which was displayed in another corner of the room. I dragged Ken over to see it.

There's something about the women that Vermeer painted that I identify with completely. I could imagine being that woman concentrating intently on the bobbins and pins with which she is making lace. Not that I can sew, you understand. It's her total involvement with what she's doing that gets me. She wears a yellow dress with a lace collar; her hair is parted in the middle, and a long curl coming out of her cap is silhouetted against the plain beige wall behind her. In front of her is a dark blue sewing cushion holding red and white threads. Her eyes are looking down at her hands making the lace, so you don't know what color they are. She is totally engrossed in her work. I'm there in that room with her in the seventeenth century.

Ken watched me dive into the painting, so absorbed in it that he probably felt invisible.

"You really like Vermeer, don't you?" he asked, interrupting my thoughts.

"There's nobody else like him," I said. "His paintings are smaller than Hals and Rembrandt's, for one thing, so I can take them in better, I think. And his subjects are always doing something. They're not just posing for a picture. They look as if they've been caught at work or talking to someone. As if they've been photographed almost."

"Didn't I read somewhere that he used a camera obscura—whatever that is—when he painted?" Ken asked.

"I try not to think about that," I said, "but I did read that he projected an image of what he was painting onto a canvas with a camera obscura and painted over that to achieve the realistic look of his subjects. I'd rather believe that he was incredibly good at what he did and didn't need any kind of device to do it. I'm an expert at suppressing facts that don't fit my idea of what I want them to be."

"What exactly is a camera obscura?" Ken asked.

"I think—and I don't really understand it," I said, "but I think it's a sort of box that reflects an image onto a piece of paper or a painter's canvas. It was used before the modern camera was invented. It's like a camera without film. Get it?"

"Not really," Ken said. "I do know what you mean about suppressing facts that you don't want to face, though. When I want to blot something out, I play music. Works every time."

"My favorite way to escape is acting," I said.

"For a couple of hours while I'm on stage I'm somebody else. My problems are the problems of my character, and they're all solved by the end of the play. All I have to worry about is making that character come alive, making the audience believe I'm her and not Janice Rogers."

"You must be really good at it," Ken said. "I'd love to see you in a play."

"I keep telling you, come to New York," I said.

"I might do that," he said.

I looked at my iPhone to see what time it was.

"Oh, Ken, I've got to get back," I said. "Thanks for coming to the Louvre with me."

"I'd spend all day long with you if I could," Ken said. "You're not like other women. You have a sort of luminous quality that shines out wherever you are."

"That's the best thing you could say to me," I said. "Sure you don't want to come back to New York to live?"

"Not even to see you every day," he said. "New York is a great city. But Paris is even better. Can't you see why I love this city?"

"Oh, yes," I said. "It's seductive. The longer you stay here, the more you want to stay here. It's an addiction."

"You got it," he said.

"The only trouble with it is that if you live here as an ex-pat, you're not really part of it. You're always an observer. You don't get caught up in the politics of the city or the country."

"Bingo," he said. "That's exactly what I love about it. I don't have to get involved."

I love to get involved in everything that interests me, right up to my eyeballs, but I didn't tell him that.

"Walk me out to the Metro, will you, Ken?"

We wound our way out of the second floor and went down the stairs to the exit from the museum.

He put me on the Metro going back to my apartment. "See you tomorrow?" he said.

"We'll see," I said. "I'm not sure how long we are going to be in Paris. Thanks for today, Ken."

Back at the apartment, I was the first one to get there. I had forty minutes to dress before Alan came for me. Since this might be my last night in this city, I wanted to look smashing. I kept pushing aside the question that wouldn't go away. Was I going to that room upstairs with him after dinner? He was so good-looking. When he held me in his arms when we were dancing, I wanted more. Why was this so hard for me? *Never mind, Scarlet,* I thought. *I'll think about that tomorrow.*

I showered, washed my hair, and was considering which dress to wear when Pat came in.

"Hey, Pat," I said. "How was your tea at the George Cinq?"

"Unbelievable, Jan," she said. She had a dreamy look on her face, which is not like Pat at all.

"Tell me about it," I said.

She sat down on the bed while I slid into my black-and-white, slinky dress, which seemed just right for this rendezvous with the unknown.

"You look incredible in that dress, Jan," she said.

"Tell me about you and Geneviève and the George Cinq," I said, brushing my hair so that it fell smoothly around both sides of my face. "What happened?"

"Jan, she's one of the most interesting woman I've ever met," Pat said. "She studied criminal law at Oxford, came back here and worked in the justice department, was appointed police captain of Paris, and has met everyone you'd ever want to meet—presidents, prime ministers, movie stars, writers, everyone."

"Is she more interesting than Denise?" I asked. I couldn't help it. We're all protective of Denise because she's our agent and a really neat lady.

"She's interesting in a different way," Pat said. "The trouble is, I'm fascinated by Geneviève's face. It's hard to look into those big blue eyes and not fall in love with her."

"And?" I asked.

"There's another woman in her life too," Pat said. "We're both committed to someone else. But Jan, she kissed me in the taxi coming back here, and it wasn't a casual kiss. It was asking me for more. I don't know what to do."

"Wow. Serious, huh?" I said, surprised at Pat's emotion.

"I'm not sure," she said. She stood up. "I'm thinking about it, though."

"I know you'll make the right decision," I said.

"Right for whom?" She smiled. "I'm meeting her later for supper and whatever."

"Hang in there, Pat. You're one of the smartest women I know."

"I don't think smart has much to do with it," she said. "I'll let you finish dressing."

She went into the other bedroom, and I put on makeup and a pair of long, dangling diamond earrings that my last husband, the rich one, had given me for Christmas one year. I didn't marry him for his money, but it didn't hurt. I'd still be with him if he hadn't tried to stop me from acting. Ironically, he fell in love with me when he saw me in a play, but after we were married, he wanted me to stay home and wait on him, give elaborate dinner parties, be available to travel with him at a moment's notice. That didn't work when I was in the middle of a long-run play, so we parted amicably, with a sense of relief on both our parts, I think. I see his photo in the *Times* Style section, accompanied by his smiling, perfectly coiffed fourth wife, surrounded by other smiling, perfectly coiffed wives and paunchy rich husbands.

Shoes. Which shoes should I wear? I had one pair of white stiletto heels, which I could hardly walk in but which made my legs look fantastic. I figured I wouldn't be doing much walking, so I put them on. They were perfect with the dress.

I hobbled into Pat's bedroom. "What do you think, Pat? Are these shoes too much?"

"They're definitely too much," she said, "but they look terrific. If you can walk in them, wear them."

Alan arrived to pick me up at seven before the other three hoofers got back from the museum. When I opened the door, he looked at me and then took me in his arms and kissed me. "You are so beautiful I want to hold you every minute I'm with you," he said.

"You'll spoil me, Alan," I said, taking his hand and pulling him to the elevator.

The limo was waiting outside the apartment.

François took us to the club and opened the door for me.

"Bon appetit, mademoiselle," he said.

"Merci, François," I said.

Chapter 12

Sleepy-Time Gal

The door of the club opened, and Ahmet bowed when he saw us. "Bonjour, Ahmet," I said to him and then froze. Now I remembered where I had seen that gold earring that Captain Chantal showed us on the bateau. The earring the police had found in Madame Fouchet's apartment the day she was killed. I had seen it in Ahmet's ear when Alan and I went there the night before. His earlobe now was bare, unearringed, guilty. I couldn't move. He must have killed Madame Fouchet and probably Monsieur Fouchet too. I remembered somebody saying they had seen Henri talking to a man with an Indian accent on the top deck just before he was murdered.

"Entrez, mademoiselle," Ahmet said. "Welcome." He was cordial, but he had seen me staring at his ear. He led the way to a table hidden away from the other tables, and said to Alan, "Champagne, monsieur?"

"Yes, Ahmet, please," Alan said, sitting down next to me. "Let's make it Dom Perignon tonight." Ahmet left to get the champagne.

"Alan," I said.

"What's the matter, Janice?" he said. "You look funny."

"Ahmet wasn't wearing his earring," I said.

Alan looked at me, confused at first and then serious. "What earring are you talking about?" he said.

"The earring he had on last night," I said. "The gold one."

"He probably just forgot to put it in tonight," Alan said and picked up the menu. "He doesn't wear it every night."

"But it's the same earring that Captain Chantal showed us on the boat," I stammered. "The one the police found in Madame Fouchet's apartment. The gold earring that Ahmet was wearing when we were here last night. You must have seen it."

"Janice, calm down," he said. "Don't get hysterical. There are thousands of earrings that look like that," Alan said. "It's just a coincidence."

Ahmet brought the champagne in an ice bucket and put it beside the table. He filled two glasses and handed them to us.

"Ahmet," Alan said, chuckling, "Madame Rogers noticed that you weren't wearing your gold earring tonight, as you usually do. She thinks you must have dropped it in Madame Fouchet's apartment when you killed her."

Ahmet almost dropped the bottle of champagne but recovered quickly. He put his hand to his ear. "Oh, I took it off when I went for my haircut this morning," he said. "I'm glad you reminded me. I'll get it back tomorrow." He put the glasses down in front of us, bowed, and went back to the kitchen.

"I must be wrong," I said. But I knew I was right. And Alan was covering up for him. It couldn't be. Alan couldn't be involved in murder—two murders actually. He was too—what?— too normal. I must be mistaken to even think that. The logical side of my brain took over: *What is normal anyway? Most killers probably look normal most of the time. Except when they're actually murdering someone.*

Alan took my chin in his hand and kissed me lightly. "A natural mistake," he said. "I've seen a lot of Indian men in Paris wearing a gold earring similar to that one."

My mind kept shouting at me, *Then why wasn't*

Ahmet wearing his tonight? The other part of my brain tried to calm me down. *Because he left it at the barber's,* it said. *Believe that and you'll believe you speak fluent French,* the crazy side said. I took a sip of the champagne.

Alan was watching me closely. "Surely you don't think I'd hire a murderer to be the host of my club," he said with a tight smile.

"Of course not, Alan," I said. "I'm obviously mistaken." I looked around the club and realized we were the only two people in the room.

"Where is everybody tonight?" I said.

"It's still early," Alan said. "Most people don't eat until eight or nine. What would you like to eat?"

"You decide," I said to him. "Anything is fine."

Alan waved to Ahmet, who was standing across the room.

"Ahmet, we'll have the shrimp bisque first and then the quail veronique. And if we have room, a chocolate soufflé for dessert."

"Oui, monsieur," he said, gathering up our menus and heading for the kitchen.

"Sounds lovely," I said. "What's veronique?"

"It means it's made with green grapes. Light and delicious. The chef browns the quails in butter, then cooks them in white wine, adds the grapes and almonds, and cooks them some more until they are tender and incredibly good. You'll love it."

Alan poured me another glass of champagne.

149

"The chef here is one of the best in Paris," he said. "I stole him from another restaurant."

"Sounds delicious," I said. I was distracted. I couldn't keep my mind on the food. I kept thinking about the earring. "Do you think Captain Chantal will let you leave for New York with Suzette this week?" I asked.

"I think it can be arranged," he said. "There's no reason for her to keep me here."

"What about Suzette's papers?" I asked. "Wasn't there a problem with her visa or something?"

"I straightened all that out," Alan said.

"Tell me about Suzette," I said. "Are you in love with her?"

"Only with her singing," he said. "She reminds people of Piaf. She's very ambitious. She thinks she'll be a big star in New York."

"And will she be?" I asked.

"Probably not," he said. "But she'll be perfect for my club."

Ahmet brought the shrimp bisque and filled our wineglasses with white wine. "A chardonnay," he said as he poured.

The soup was exquisite. I couldn't believe I was still hungry after the lunch we had eaten in Giverny, but nobody could resist this bisque.

"Oh, Alan, what's in this?" I asked.

"Besides the shrimp, some mushrooms, celery, cayenne, nutmeg, wine, chicken stock, and heavy cream, pureed until heavenly."

He took a spoonful of his bisque and then watched me finish mine.

"You're not eating yours?" I asked.

"I'm not really hungry," he said. "Except to hold you. Dance with me."

He stood up and held out his hand. I started to get up and sat back down again. I felt a little dizzy.

"Are you all right?" he asked.

"I think so," I said. "I just felt odd there for a minute. As if I were going to fall down."

He took both my hands in his and helped me stand up. "Too much champagne, perhaps?" he said. I had only had one glass.

The music was all French songs this evening. As Alan put his arms around me, I recognized Charles Trenet's voice singing "La Romance de Paris." I closed my eyes and leaned against him. I was getting sleepier and sleepier. Weird, because I had often had longer days than this and was wide awake until dawn. I hadn't had much to drink. I tried to fight it, but I felt myself passing out in his arms.

Mary McHugh

RECIPES FOR SHRIMP BISQUE AND QUAIL VERONIQUE

Shrimp Bisque

Serves six.

2 lbs. shrimp, shelled, de-veined, and diced
½ cup chopped mushrooms
4 tbsps. butter
3 cups chicken stock
1 cup dry white wine
1 stalk celery
⅛ tsp. cayenne pepper
⅛ tsp. nutmeg
1 cup heavy cream
Whipped cream

1. Sauté the shrimp and mushrooms in the butter in a saucepan for five minutes.
2. Add stock and wine
3. Mix in celery, cayenne, and nutmeg.
4. Cook over low heat for twenty minutes.
5. Take out the celery and puree the mixture.
6. Put the soup back in the saucepan.
7. Add the heavy cream and stir.
8. When very hot, plop some whipped cream on top and serve.

Quail Veronique

Serves six.

6 quails
3 tbsps. flour
2½ tsps. salt
½ tsp. white pepper
5 tbsps. butter
¾ cup dry white wine
¾ cup seedless green grapes
4 tbsps. blanched, sliced almonds

1. Mix the salt and pepper with the flour.
2. Dip the quails in the flour, salt, and pepper.
3. Brown the quails in the butter in a deep skillet.
4. Add wine, cover, and cook for about fifteen minutes over low heat.
5. Add grapes and almonds.
6. Cook until quails are tender, about five minutes.

Janice's Fashion Tip: Want to look Parisian? Wear black with a colorful scarf or a gold necklace.

Chapter 13

Help!!!!

I woke up in bed in a dark room, coughing and gasping for breath. Where was I? The smell of chlorine was strong. I had to get out of there. I could barely move. I managed to roll out of the bed and crawl across the room to the door. I reached up and pulled on the knob to open it, but it wouldn't budge. I staggered to my feet and pulled, but the door was sealed.

I was having a lot of trouble breathing. There was a window on the other side of the room. I crawled over to it and tried to open it, but it too was sealed shut. I was just about to pass out again when I realized there was another closed door next to the bed. I could see a light underneath it. I had just enough strength to try the handle, which, miraculously, turned. I was in the bathroom. I dragged myself in there and closed the door again. The smell of chlorine was only barely noticeable in there. I saw a rack of towels next to the tub and grabbed a couple of them to stuff under the door. I wet a wash cloth with cold water and put it around my mouth and nose. My throat and eyes stung. I lay on the floor for a moment and then looked around for a window. There was a small one on the far wall. I pulled myself up by one of the towel racks and reached the window.

It was sealed. I had to wake up. I crawled to the sink and turned on the cold water and let it wash over my head and face. Little by little, I regained enough consciousness to figure out a plan. I had to break the window and climb out of there.

I dried my face and hair and glanced around the room. What could I break the glass with? My shoe? No, I wasn't wearing shoes. I was still dressed, but my stilettos were gone. I looked in the cabinet under the sink for something, anything, heavy enough to break the window. A hair dryer. That might do it. No, too small. Next to the sink was a metal wastebasket. That would work. I could smash the glass with that and get out of there.

With the last bit of strength left in me, I heaved the wastebasket against the window and shattered it. The cool night air revived me. The question was, could I fit through that window? It was kind of small, but I thought I could do it. Then what? How high up was I? I peered out and realized I was on the second floor of the club. The back of the club. There was an open Dumpster, full of the night's garbage and trash, right under me. All I had to do was jump into that mess. Right.

I knocked out the jagged pieces of glass still in the window with the wastebasket, put a towel over the sill to sit on, climbed up on the clothes hamper, eased my way out, and jumped. I landed on something soft and mushy. Oh, ick. Somebody hadn't finished his chocolate soufflé. Well, I could have landed in worse stuff. There was nobody around. I wriggled over the edge of the Dumpster. Now what? I realized I didn't have my purse, which had my phone in it. And my money. It was back there in that room.

I had to get out of there. To my right I could see a narrow street. I stumbled toward it, my bare feet scraping against gravel. There was nobody around. I had no idea what time it was, but I figured it must be late to be so deserted. Ah, a sign. Rue de Rennes. I actually knew where I was because I had walked this way with Ken the other day. This street led to Boulevard Raspail, which led to Boulevard du Montparnasse and our apartment. All I had to do was walk barefoot to safety. That's all. Every step hurt.

I tried to figure out what had happened. One minute I was eating shrimp bisque and drinking a glass of chardonnay, and the next I was in a room filled with chlorine gas. How did that happen? My mind was still foggy. Alan! I was dancing with Alan. I vaguely remembered falling asleep in his arms. I didn't have that much to drink. There must have been something in the shrimp bisque that knocked me out. Why? Of course. It was because I mentioned Ahmet's earring to Alan. Alan must have been the one who drugged me. He and Ahmet were working together. Why didn't I realize that before? When I noticed that Ahmet wasn't wearing the earring, I was stupid enough to mention it to Alan. They must have knocked me out and carried me up to that room, sealed it, and filled it with chlorine gas. They knew I might figure out that Alan hired Ahmet to kill Monsieur and Madame Fouchet so he could take Suzette to New York. They tried to kill me too!

Alan a killer? He seemed so nice. I could just hear Gini if I told her that. "All killers seem nice,

Jan. Until they strangle someone and cut up their body parts and store them in the fridge. They don't wear signs saying, 'I'm a killer.' "

I trudged along, stumbling, almost falling, my feet sore and bleeding. Rue de Rennes. Rue Notre-Dame des Champs. Rue Vavin. And finally Boulevard du Montparnasse and our apartment.

Janice's Fashion Tip: If someone is trying to kill you, run. Don't worry about the chocolate soufflé all over your dress.

Chapter 14

What Chlorine Gas?

I could barely see, but I managed to punch in the code that opened the door of the building. I don't know how I remembered anything at that point. I made it to the elevator, got off at the third floor, and realized I had no key to get into the apartment. It was back at the club in my purse. I had no idea what time it was, but I had no other choice than to bang on the door until I woke someone.

My first attempts were too weak to wake a nervous cat, but I kept at it until I heard Mary Louise's voice asking, "Who's there?"

I said "It's Jan. Let me in." I sounded hoarse, not like myself.

Mary Louise opened the door a crack and gasped when she saw me crumpled on the floor.

"Jan, what happened to you? Here, let me help you." She opened the door, reached under my arms, and pulled me into the apartment. I couldn't move. She ran to get the pillow from her sofa bed and put it under my head. "You have no shoes. Where have you been? Are you all right? I'll make you some coffee."

She ran into the kitchen and turned on the coffeemaker that was loaded for breakfast and came back to kneel next to me.

"Can you talk? Oh, Jan, you look awful. Your feet are all torn up. Wait, I'll get you my slippers."

She reached under the sofa bed and pulled out her feathery pink slippers and put them on my feet. She knelt down again beside me and smoothed back my hair.

"What time is it?" I asked.

"Five o'clock," she said. "Where were you?"

"Alan tried to kill me," I said.

"What do you mean, he tried to kill you," she said. "That nice man tried to kill you?"

"Don't let Gini hear you say that," I said and started to laugh, but the laughing made me cough. I couldn't stop.

Mary Louise ran into the kitchenette and

poured me a glass of water from the bottle in the fridge.

"Here, drink this. The coffee's almost ready."

I took a few sips of the water until I could talk again. I was exhausted. I only had enough strength to tell Mary Louise the basic story of Ahmet and the earring, eating this incredible shrimp bisque with Alan, dancing with him, waking up in a room filled with chlorine gas, breaking the window and escaping, walking home with no shoes.

"Did you get the recipe for the shrimp bisque?" she asked. We both started laughing so hard, the door to one of the bedrooms opened and Gini stumbled out.

"Do you realize what time it is?" she said in typical Gini fashion, not noticing that I was lying on the floor with no shoes on and chocolate soufflé all over the side of my dress.

This made Mary Louise and me laugh even more until Gini took another look at me.

"Jan, what happened to you? Are you all right? What's that all over your dress?"

There I was, almost killed, lying on the floor of the apartment, and she was worried about my dress.

"Alan tried to kill her," Mary Louise said.

"What do you mean, he tried to kill her?" Gini said, echoing Mary Louise. It was almost impossible to believe that the handsome, successful, kind man who took us to Giverny to see the water lilies and Monet's house could turn out to be a murderer.

I told her my abbreviated version of the whole ghastly night.

"We have to call Captain Chantal right away," Gini said, "before he gets away."

"At five in the morning?" I said. "She'll be asleep." I was still obviously not thinking clearly.

"Jan!" Gini said. "Cops are used to being awakened at all hours. That's their job. The sooner she gets over to that club, the sooner she'll get him. What if he's on his way to the airport right now? Stay there. I'll call her."

I wasn't going anywhere. I couldn't move. I wondered if the chocolate soufflé would come out of my dress. It was one of my favorites. I could be lying back in that club dead forever, and here I was worrying about my dress. What was wrong with me? Maybe the mind does this after traumatic events to protect us from going into shock. It concentrates on frivolous things. I'd have to ask Pat, our psychologist and counselor.

Speaking of Pat, her bedroom door opened, and she and Tina hurried across the living room to kneel down beside me.

"Jan," Tina said. "Honey, what happened? You look terrible."

"Gini, you tell them," I said. I couldn't bear to go through the whole thing again.

Mary Louise went to pour coffee for all of us while Gini told them my grisly tale.

"Did you call the police?" Pat asked.

"I was just about to do that," Gini said.

"Let me," Pat said. "Geneviève gave me her cell phone number. I know she would want me to call her."

Pat went into her bedroom to get her phone and make the call.

"She's on her way over here," Pat said when she came back. "Do you feel up to talking to her?"

"Sure," I said. "Help me into that chair over there and give me a cup of coffee. I'll be okay." I wasn't sure I'd ever be okay again.

Captain Chantal knocked on our door twenty minutes later, accompanied by two police officers. She was in uniform and looked as if she had been up and working for hours.

"Are you all right, Madame Rogers?" she asked.

"Call me Janice," I said. "I'm not all right. I may never be all right again, but I can tell you what happened." I gave her the fast version of my story.

"I sent two of my men over to the club to arrest Monsieur Anderson and Ahmet after I talked to Pat on the phone," the captain said. "I need a few more details."

"I'll try," I said. "I'm still not thinking too clearly."

"I understand," she said. "Did you say the room was filled with chlorine gas?"

"That's what it smelled like," I said. "My throat and nose were burning, and I could barely breathe. If that bathroom hadn't been there, I wouldn't be talking to you now."

"You escaped by breaking the window with a metal wastebasket. Correct?"

"Right," I said. "I was lucky it was there."

"There was a full Dumpster right under the window that you jumped into?"

"Yes," I said. "That's how I got this chocolate stuff all over my dress."

The captain took out her phone and photographed my dress.

"You also reported that the man who acts as maître d' at this club is Indian and that he was not wearing the gold earring he had been wearing the night before when you were there. And that the gold earring looked like the one I showed you on the boat after the murder of Madame Fouchet."

"That's right," I said. "I mentioned it to Alan, and that's why they tried to kill me."

"Please rest," she said. "I will question them now, and when you're up to it, I will talk to you again."

"Of course, Captain Chantal," I said. "I'm surprised he and Ahmet are still at the club. I would have thought they would have left the country."

"That surprises me too," she said.

She left the apartment with the two officers.

My friends helped me into bed, where I fell into a deep sleep for a couple of hours.

When I woke up, I felt much better. My feet were sore, but that was only temporary.

My friends were still in the apartment, and Mary Louise was making mushroom omelets for us.

"You look much better," Tina said and led me to a chair at the table. She handed me a glass of orange juice, some omelet, and a cup of hot coffee. I was so relieved to be alive, I was actually hungry and dove into the omelet, which was delicious. I had just buttered my croissant and taken a sip of the hot, reviving coffee when there was a knock on our door.

Gini opened it, and Captain Chantal was standing there with two other police officers. She looked very serious.

"I'm sorry to disturb you again so soon, Madame—um—Janice," she said, "but I had a very confusing interview with Monsieur Anderson."

"Confusing?" I said. "What he did is pretty clear."

"I certainly thought so after talking to you, but now I have many questions."

"Like what?" I said, losing my appetite again.

The captain took out her iPad and checked her notes. "Monsieur Anderson said you drank too much champagne and wine and that you passed out at the table. He said he carried you upstairs to the bedroom so you could sleep it

off, and then he was going to take you home.
But when he went to look for you an hour later,
you had left, and he assumed you came back to
the apartment."

"No, no, that's not what happened at all," I
said, talking too fast, my mind racing to correct
this absurd description of what happened. I told
her again about being drugged, about the chlorine gas, the sealed door and windows, my breaking the window in the bathroom and jumping out
to land in the full Dumpster.

"Yes, I know," the captain said. "But when I
took Monsieur Anderson back to the club,
Ahmet was there, wearing a gold earring, by the
way, which was similar to the one we found in
Madame Fouchet's apartment but not exactly
like it. Monsieur Anderson took us up to the
bedroom. The door opened readily. There was
not a trace of chlorine gas in the room. Your
purse was still on the table by the bed, untouched.
Your shoes were right there. My officers have
them and will return them to you. The bathroom was neat. The window was not broken and
opened easily. I looked down at the ground beneath the bathroom window and there was no
Dumpster there. Is it possible that you dreamed
all this?"

I could not speak. I stared at her, my mouth
open, trying to answer her. Finally, I managed to
say, "Dreamed it? How could I have dreamed it?
If I left the club by the front door, how come no-

body saw me leave? Why wouldn't I have looked for Alan and asked him to drive me home?"

"Monsieur Anderson was puzzled by this as well. He said the few customers they had that night had already left. He and Ahmet were still at the club, but they must have been in the kitchen when you left. He didn't understand why you didn't come to find him. He said he was very worried about you, and went to find you in the bedroom about an hour later but you had left. He was going to call you this morning to make sure you were all right."

"I did not dream it," I said. Then I thought, *What if I did? What if I was drunk? What if I made the whole thing up? No, I could not have made up the chocolate soufflé all over my dress. It is still there.*

"You can see the chocolate soufflé on my dress from landing in the Dumpster," I said.

"Monsieur Anderson had an answer for that too," Geneviève said. "He said he didn't mean to embarrass you, but before you passed out, you tried to eat your dessert—the chocolate soufflé the club is famous for—but you knocked it off the table and it fell on your dress. Then you became unconscious, and he carried you upstairs."

"Then there should have been chocolate soufflé all over the sheets I was lying on," I said.

"He said they had to change the sheets after he went up to check on you because someone was scheduled to use the room the next day."

"Did you ask to see the dirty sheets?" I asked.

"They had already been washed and put away by the time we got there," she said. "Listen, Janice. I know you wouldn't lie. But when people have too much to drink, they sometimes hallucinate and imagine all kinds of things. There is no sign in that club that you were gassed or broke a window and jumped out into a Dumpster. Monsieur Anderson was very cooperative. He said he liked you very much and was sorry he had given you too much to drink."

I could not believe what I was hearing. The whole experience had been erased. There was not a wisp of evidence to prove that I had almost died in that room, that I knew who did it, that I had not just imagined the whole thing.

I looked at my friends' faces. Their expressions were concerned, somewhat confused. I didn't know whether they believed what Captain Chantal was telling them or what I had told them. To be honest, I was wavering back and forth between the two versions myself.

But every time I began to think that maybe I had been drunk, had hallucinated, I knew that chlorine gas was real. I remembered breaking that window with the wastebasket. I felt the jolt of landing in that Dumpster again. It could not have been a dream. How was I going to prove it?

"Captain Chantal," I said, "Monsieur Anderson was lying to you. I was not hallucinating. I know he tried to kill me. Could you please investigate that room and bathroom again? There must be some clue. Maybe some bits of glass on the floor in the bathroom that were overlooked when you first went there. Maybe some small pieces of whatever they used to seal the door and windows are still there. Somebody in one of the buildings in back of the club might have seen me jump, or heard something, or saw the Dumpster there earlier. I did not imagine all this."

"Geneviève," Pat said, coming to sit on the arm of my chair, "Janice is not a drunk. She doesn't pass out after a glass of wine or two. Something was in that wine or in her food to knock her out."

"She doesn't make things up," Tina said. "If she woke up in a room filled with chlorine gas, that was no dream. There has to be some clue in that bedroom or bathroom that will prove what she's saying is true."

"You can't just let Anderson and that Indian guy go," Gini said. "They might try to kill Jan again. You've got to believe her. She's not some flake who dreams up whole murder plots against her. She's a totally reliable person."

My eyes filled with tears. I looked around the room at those loyal friends and thanked God that they were in my life.

Captain Chantal put down her iPad. "I believe you," she said. "I'll send a team back to that room and examine every inch of it. There must be something left in there that will prove your story. We'll find it—don't worry. In the meantime, I want you to spend this day out of the city. I'll send a police officer to pick you up in a van and take you anywhere you want to go as long as it's away from Paris. I can't let Monsieur Anderson leave the country until this case is solved. He might try to kill you again."

I shivered. "Thank you, Captain," I said. "I am very grateful."

Geneviève stood up and moved toward the door, but paused and looked around. She sighed.

"I love this building," she said. She started to say something else and then stopped.

"What is it, Geneviève?" Pat said.

"Oh, it was such a long time ago," the captain said. "But I'll never forget it. My first girlfriend lived in this building. We were only fifteen, but we loved each other. She was funny and smart and we wanted to be alone, which wasn't easy with both our parents checking up on us all the time. So Catherine found this room on the ground floor, hidden way in the back, that used to belong to the concierge when the building had one. No one knew it was there. We used to go there in the afternoons and do our homework together and fool around." She stopped, embarrassed.

"It's all right, Geneviève," Pat said. "There's nothing to be ashamed of. Tell us about it."

The captain sat down on the arm of one of the chairs, her mind back in those days of youthful love. "She called me Genève when we were in that room," she said. "It's the only place she called me that. And no one else used that name. We didn't want anyone to know about us or that room. I think it's still there, but I haven't been back in years."

"What happened to Catherine?" Pat asked.

"She went to Oxford too," Geneviève said. "She married a Brit before she got her degree and stayed in England. She stopped writing to me after she got married."

The captain looked around at all of us, her eyes lingering on Pat. "I really loved her," she said. "Every time I come to this building I remember her."

We were silent. I felt like we were intruding on a secret part of her life.

She stood up and snapped back into this time and place.

"I will investigate that club again, Jan," she said.

She left.

"You guys are the best," I said. "Thank you for believing me. I almost didn't believe me myself when she told me how completely Alan had cleaned up after I left. I don't know how he did it so fast and so completely."

"We know you, Jan," Gini said. "There's no way you could have imagined all that. Now all we have to do is keep you alive until they arrest Anderson and Ahmet."

"That might take a while," I said.

My phone rang. "Hello," I said.

"My dear Janice, are you all right?" It was Alan Anderson.

I started to shake. I almost dropped the phone. I mouthed "Alan Anderson" to my friends.

"I was really worried when I went back to the room and you were gone," he said. "I thought you would sleep for hours. You were really out. You should have come to find me when you woke up. I would have driven you back to your apartment. Are you sure you're all right?" His voice was concerned. Anybody except me would have thought he had nothing to do with trying to kill me just a few hours before.

"I'm fine, Alan," I said, my voice almost normal. I wasn't going to let him know that I knew he had tried to kill me. Good thing I've been an actress all these years. "Sorry I passed out on you. I don't usually do that."

"Not to worry," he said. "Maybe you shouldn't have so much wine the next time. I always assume everyone can drink as much as I can, but that's not always true for women."

I marveled at his tone. The next time? Whoaaa. There ain't gonna be no next time for me, as the song says. "Guess I'll stick to fruit juice from now on," I said. "Thanks for checking on me, Alan."

"Let me know if I can do anything for you," he said.

Sure I will, I thought. *You can go directly to jail. Do not pass Go.*

"Good-bye for now," he said and hung up.

"Was that really Anderson?" Tina asked.

"Can you believe that guy?" I asked.

"What did he say?" Gini asked.

"He's worried about me and wants to be sure I'm all right!" I said. "Maybe this really is a dream, and I'll wake up soon and laugh about it."

"Every time you start to laugh, take a look at your dress," Gini said. "That'll convince you."

"He scares me," Mary Louise said. "Let's get out of the city, like Geneviève said. Where shall we go?"

"Come on, somebody, come up with a really good plan," Gini said. "I'll go anywhere."

"I have an idea," Mary Louise said in her excuse-me-this-is-probably-a-terrible-idea voice. "We could go to Versailles. Both times I've been in Paris I've wanted to go there, but we never had the time. If you've all seen it enough, never mind. It was just a thought."

"That's a great idea, Weezy," Gini said, using the nickname just to annoy Mary Louise. She hates it. "They've totally redone Versailles since I was there the last time," Gini said. "I could get some great shots there."

"Let's go there," Tina said. "I read somewhere that they have musical fountain shows in the afternoon, with music and water shooting out of the fountains."

"You guys go ahead," Pat said. "I've seen Versailles, and I told Geneviève I'd meet her later this afternoon."

"It's fine with me," I said. I was ready to get as far away from the city and Alan Anderson as I could get. "Just let me change my clothes and I'll be ready."

"You sure you're up to this?" Mary Louise, our mother hen, said. "You've been through hell."

"I'm up for anything that gets me out of here," I said.

I squirmed out of my dress and took a long, hot shower. Every inch of me felt dirty and sore. The shower helped a lot. I changed into a blue-and-white halter top and striped jeans and joined the rest of my gang, who were ready to go.

Chapter 15

What Do You Mean— Perfumed Lambs?

We only had to wait a few minutes before the police van pulled up in front of the building. A friendly-faced officer got out of the van and introduced himself.

"Bonjour, mesdames," he said. "I am here to take you wherever you want to go and to help you in any way I can. My name is Jacques Paulhe, at your service."

He was such a sweetheart. I was grateful to Geneviève for sending him to us.

"We'd like to go to Versailles, please, Officer Paulhe," Gini said. "Is that OK with you?"

"Always," he said. "And I will be able to get you in ahead of the line. It's very busy there in July."

"We would also like to stay to see the musical fountain show in the afternoon," Tina said. "Can you spend that much time with us?"

He smiled. "I would gladly spend every day with such charming and beautiful ladies," he said.

Did I mention I love the French? Especially the men.

We bustled into the van, which was air-conditioned and roomy, and settled in for the half-hour drive to Versailles.

Officer Paulhe entertained us the whole way with things we absolutely must not miss in Paris. He obviously loved his city, and he wanted us to see everything.

"Be sure to go to the Rodin museum," he said. "Especially the garden. It's an experience to see those huge, black sculptures that are so famous outside. *The Kiss, The Thinker.* And go to the top of the Arc de Triomphe. Most people don't know they are allowed to do that. Such a view of all the avenues flowing out from the Arc. It's a lesson in how to plan a city to emphasize its beauty. It's why people love to come here. Everywhere you look there is something to surprise you with its elegance."

It was a treat to hear him talk about Paris. He drove effortlessly in and out of traffic jams as we left the city, smoothly and quickly on the high-way leading to Versailles.

"Oh, and mesdames," he said, "I know every-one tells you it is just for tourists, but you must eat at the Eiffel Tower. They have two restau-rants, a very expensive one called the Jules Verne, and one that's more affordable and very good too called 58 Tour Eiffel. And if you can, eat at La Tour d'Argent, also expensive but worth it for the view of Notre-Dame and the Seine and for the way they treat you as if you are the only cus-tomer they have."

"Tourist traps," Gini muttered, way too knowl-edgeable about Parisian restaurants to go where everybody else went.

I gave her my fierce shut-up-Gini look, which sometimes works and sometimes doesn't. This time it worked.

Officer Paulhe swung into the fast lane and continued his commentary.

"If you're into cemeteries, there's one near you that has lots of famous people buried there. It's the Cimetière du Montparnasse. Simone de Beauvoir and Jean-Paul Sartre are there—still together in death." He chuckled. "And there's Samuel Beckett, Guy de Maupassant, Saint-Saëns. Even Susan Sontag is there. An Ameri-can. Did you know her?"

"Afraid not, Officer Paulhe," Gini said. "Not all Americans know each other."

This time I punched her and glared at her. I

liked this friendly policeman, and I wasn't going to let Gini sneer at him.

"Of course, if you want a really impressive tomb, you must go to Les Invalides, where Napoleon is buried. They often have concerts there."

"I once fell off one of the smaller tombs in there next to Napoleon when there weren't enough chairs during a concert," Gini said. "I fell asleep and tumbled off onto the floor. Some lady thought I had fainted and gave me her chair and a pill, which I swallowed because I didn't want to offend her. No telling what was in it."

"Oh, mademoiselle," Officer Paulhe said, "it's not good to sit on the tombs." He seemed shocked.

"Maybe tombs are too sad for you to see," he said, cheering up again. "You should go to the zoo in the Bois de Vincennes. They've just spent six years reconstructing it so the animals aren't in cages any more. They roam about outside. There are fences to protect the people who come to see them, but the animals have a natural environment to live in. Lots of giraffes and birds and monkeys. I take my children there often."

"How many children do you have, Officer Paulhe?" Tina asked. She always asks people about their families. It's one of the reasons she's such a good travel editor. She finds out what people want to do when they go on holiday with their children and then writes about where to find it.

"Three, madame," he said. "They are all teen-agers."

Before Gini could tell this lovely man that she didn't believe in zoos, no matter how natural their environment, we arrived at Versailles.

"Et voilà, mesdames," Paulhe said. "Nous sommes ici." In other words, "We are here."

"I have instructed the security people here to watch over you," he said. "Call me when you are ready to return to Paris, and I will meet you here."

We thanked him and tumbled out of the van.

Even though I had visited Versailles on my honeymoon with Derek, I was overwhelmed again by the size of the palace.

"Can you believe this was once a hunting lodge?" Gini said.

"I'd forgotten that," Tina said. "It was Louis the Fourteenth who turned it into this incredi-ble place, right?"

"Right," Gini said, "but he didn't stop there. He built the Grand Trianon, another smaller palace, for his mistress Madame de Maintenon. Louis the Fifteenth and Louis the Sixteenth added on to that. The furnishings are mostly from Napoleon's time. I don't know if we can see it all, but let's try."

"What I remember most," I said, "are the

enormous formal gardens and pools and statues in back of the main palace. They went on for miles. You could never see the whole thing."

"How about starting in the main palace," Gini said. "Should we take a tour so we know what we're looking at? It's huge."

"Yes, let's do that," Mary Louise said. "English-speaking, please."

"You mean I haven't taught you enough French to take the French-speaking tour?" Gini asked. She loves to tease Mary Louise.

"Pas encore, ma chérie," Mary Louise said, surprising us all with her "Not yet, my dear."

"Alors!" Gini said. "Très bien, Weezy."

We signed up for the next available tour, and within fifteen minutes we were greeted by a chic, dark-haired woman wearing a white sleeveless dress with a pleated skirt.

"You are Americans, no?" she asked, her accent charming and delightful to the ear.

"We are Americans, yes," Gini answered. "Only one of us speaks French—me—so we need you to speak to us in English, please."

"Of course," she said. "My name is Annette. Feel free to ask questions at any time."

We followed her into the main palace's Hall of Mirrors, a room decorated in crystal and glass that was even more stunning than when I had seen it twenty-five years earlier.

"Jan, doesn't this remind you of the Great

Hall in Catherine the Great's summer palace—
the one we saw in Russia," Tina asked me.

"You're right, Tina!" I said. "All glass and gold
and sparkle."

"This room was originally built by Louis the
Fourteenth, the Sun King, in the seventeenth
century, as a meeting place for people who came
to see him, for celebrations, to impress foreign
royalty and ambassadors, and as a magnificent
passageway from one part of the palace to another," Annette said. "It was restored in 2007 at a
cost of twelve million euros, or sixteen million
dollars. It is 236 feet long. There are 357 mirrors, and seventeen arches opposite seventeen
windows. Each arch has twenty-one mirrors.
When the mirrors were restored, only forty-
eight of them had to be replaced. The others
were put in place when Louis the Fourteenth
built the palace. They are a bit smoky and distorted in places, but it's amazing that they have
been here since 1684.

"You will notice the paintings on the ceiling.
They show Louis the Fourteenth's military victo-
ries in the seventeenth century. Charles Le Brun
painted some of them and supervised the painting of the others.

"This room is also historically famous because
the treaty that ended World War One was signed
here.

"Feel free to walk around and enjoy the view

of the gardens reflected in the mirrors. You may take photographs. When you're ready, we'll go to the king's apartments."

On this hot July day, the sunlight reflected in 357 mirrors made this room, with all its chandeliers and mirrors, a vast sparkling wonderland. Each crystal and each mirror looked like it had just been Windexed to within an inch of its life. I loved the bronze sculptures that held the standing chandeliers, some of cherubs holding up the light, some of robed goddesses brightening the room.

When my eyes grew tired of the unceasingly bright glare in this room, I looked around for my friends and saw them standing by the enormous golden carved doors at one end of the Hall of Mirrors with Annette, waiting for me. I hurried up to them and said, "What next?"

"We go to the king's Grand Apartment," Annette said. "And *grand* is definitely the word for these rooms. Follow me, and I will show you what it was like to be the man the French believed was chosen by God to be king."

We walked with her through a whole series of rooms—the Hercules salon, with a huge painting by François Lemoyne of Hercules in a chariot; the Abundance salon, where tea and liqueurs were served to guests in the afternoon; the Venus salon; the Diana salon, which Annette told us was the billiard room, where ladies were invited to watch the king play and to applaud him. "He was actually very good at it," Annette said. Then there was the Mars salon; the Mercury salon, where Louis XIV died in 1715 after ruling for seventy-two years; the Salon of War, graced by a painting of the Sun King on horseback, defeating his enemies; and finally the Apollo salon.

We were awed by the king's bedchamber, which was elaborately decorated with paintings and sculpture and hung with heavy red and gold drapes around an enormous canopied and gilded bed.

We talked in whispers in the Royal Chapel, all marble and gold, where Louis XVI and the Austrian-born Marie Antoinette were married when they were teenagers. Annette told us something called a Cliquot organ played when the king went to ten o'clock mass every day, and the greatest voices in the kingdom sang motets to soothe him.

"Well, he was chosen by God, after all," Gini said in what was for her a low voice.

Annette led us into the Clock Room. "This is Passemant's astronomical clock," she said. "It took him twenty years to make and was finished in 1753. It's supposed to keep time until the year 9999. Mozart gave a concert in this room at the age of seven."

I was beginning to weary of all this pomp and gold and heavy sculpture and paintings of wars

and gods and goddesses, so it was with some relief that Annette asked us if we would like to see
the gardens in back of Versailles.

We were all ready for the outdoors, even though
it was a hot day. The word *gardens* does not begin
to describe what Louis XIV had done with his
backyard. We walked out the heavy doors to acres
of carefully manicured lawns, flower beds,
straight paths for visitors to use, which actually
had names, and groves. In the middle of all this
beauty were two vast pools, holding elaborate
fountains with sculptures representing the four
seasons.

Annette described them to us. "That one is
Bacchus, surrounded by dragons and leaves and
vines, representing autumn. Over there is the
Saturn fountain, with an old man symbolizing
winter, with little cupids all around him."

She led us to the Flora fountain. "Flora was
the goddess of spring. There are flowers and
fruit and more cherubs around her. And summer is represented by the Ceres fountain; she
was the goddess of harvest and corn. But these
are only a few of the fountains here. There's the
Apollo fountain, with horses galloping and crash-
ing through the water, pulling him along. Apollo
was the Sun God, and Louis believed he was his
descendant. There's Neptune, with a dragon
and a jet that rises seven meters into the air.
That large fountain over there is called the La-

tona fountain. She is Apollo's mother, and she is protecting all her children from harm."

While Annette showed us the fountains, Gini was flitting about, taking pictures of everything that moved or didn't move in the garden. I was beginning to wilt from walking around in the heat.

"Annette," Tina said, "maybe we should get something to eat and then see the Grand and Petit Trianon afterward. They're about a half hour's walk from here, right? What do you say, gang? Ready to sit down for a while, have a cold drink, and eat something?"

"I thought you'd never ask," I said. "Let's go."

"Annette, will you join us for some lunch?" Tina, always the gracious hostess, asked.

"I have another group waiting for me," she said. "I'll come back for you later. Ça va?"

"Ça definitely va," Tina said.

Annette steered us toward the brasserie nearby and waved good-bye.

There were tables outside of the restaurant, but we were all hot and sweaty and went inside to the welcome air-conditioned room. We found a table for four and gulped down the water at our place settings.

"I'm so glad we did this," Mary Louise said. "It's even more beautiful since they redid the whole place."

"Wait till you see Marie Antoinette's little

farm this afternoon," Gini said. "There's also a daytime water fountain show with music, but if you're up for it, we could stay to see the nighttime show with fireworks, music, lights, and water shooting up into the air. It's really worth seeing. What do you say?"

"Let's see how we feel later," our practical Tina said. "Right now, I'm hungry and glad to be sitting down and out of that heat."

The menu promised all kinds of good things. I finally settled on the savory soufflé roll filled with mushrooms, spinach, ham, and cream cheese that Gini recommended. She ordered that too. Tina was in the mood for the crêpes with mushroom and bacon filling, and Mary Louise chose the shrimp, oranges, and anchovy salad.

"So have you guys called home since we've been here?" Tina asked. "What's happening? Gini, how's Alex?"

Gini smiled. Her face always changed from alert, constantly observing, to relaxed and happy whenever anyone mentioned Alex. She met him when we danced on the cruise ship in Russia when he was head of *The New York Times'* Moscow bureau. They connected instantly, and he later went back to the New York office of the *Times* as a columnist so he could be near Gini. They talked about getting married, but something always came up to delay it.

"He's great, Tina," Gini said. "I miss him. "He's

trying to set up a trip for us to go to India to arrange for me to adopt that little girl I met in the orphanage when I filmed a documentary there. Her name is Amalia. I know I've told you how difficult it is for a foreigner to adopt an Indian child, but Alex is determined to find a way. He's in touch with some correspondents from the *Times* who work there."

Tina reached over and squeezed Gini's hand. "If anyone can do it, Alex can," she said. "I hope it works out, Gini. I know how much you want that little girl."

"She's so bright, Tina," Gini said, tears in her eyes. "I want to take her all over the world and give her a wonderful life."

"You'll figure out how to do it, Gini," Mary Louise said. "You always do." She took a bite of her salad. "Ohhh, try this. It's fantastic."

My soufflé roll was a total delight, as were Tina's crêpes. We passed our plates around for each other to taste.

"Would you guys be embarrassed if I asked for the recipes?" Mary Louise asked. "Or rather, Gini, would you be embarrassed to ask?"

"I'm used to you, Weezy," Gini said. "They speak perfect English, of course, but if you want, I'll ask them in French."

"Would you?" Mary Louise asked. Nobody can ever resist Mary Louise. You always feel she asks for so little, how could you refuse her some little thing like that?

When the waiter appeared to refill our water glasses, Gini asked him in French if we could have the recipes for our dishes. He nodded and left to get the recipes.

We finished our lunches and had a cup of coffee; refreshed, recipes in Mary Louise's purse, and ready for the Grand and Petit Trianons, we called Annette, who joined us.

"As you probably know," she said, "the Grand Trianon was built in 1670 by Louis the Fourteenth as a place away from the main palace where he could relax with his mistress Madame de Montespan. It's quite beautiful, with pink marble arches and a magnificent formal rose garden in back. The furnishings are almost all from Napoleon's time.

"The Petit Trianon was built by Louis the Fifteenth in 1768 as his own love nest with Madame de Pompadour until she died, and then he invited Madame du Barry to move into the bedroom upstairs. When Louis the Sixteenth became king, his wife, Marie Antoinette, took it over as her own private refuge. She made it into her own special little palace to go to when she was tired of all the pomp and ceremony at the main palace. She was only nineteen when she married Louis, so this was sort of her playhouse. Only her friends were allowed to join her there. She kept the servants as inconspicuous as possible so she could pretend she was just a simple little shepherdess tending to her lambs, which were perfumed. In the back was what she called her *hameau*, or "hamlet," to bounce around in. It was an actual farm with a mill and everything. It has its own temple of love—a sort of gazebo outside—but grander, with Corinthian columns."

"Perfumed lambs!" Gini said. "That's some farm."

"I'll take you through the Petit Trianon first," Annette said. "If you're still willing, we'll go to the Grand Trianon later. I know it's quite hot today, so I don't want to wear you out."

"We'll let you know, Annette," Tina said.

Annette led us through the Petit Trianon, a charming little palace, beautifully decorated with marble and brass, magnificent paintings and sculpture, and the sweetest bed, which had a canopy with a cover of dark blue dots on a white background.

We admired the mill and gazebo outside, imagining the young, doomed queen on swings, picking flowers, feeding the animals, playing at being a normal person.

"How do you feel about going through the Grand Trianon?" Annette asked.

We looked at each other. Did we want to traipse through another palace? I didn't really, but I didn't want to spoil it for everyone else.

Gini, as usual, spoke for all of us. "Maybe we'll skip that one, Annette. I'd like to see one of the fountain shows before we go, and then I think we've had it for the day."

We were all relieved and followed Annette back to the pools in back of the main palace.

One of the water fountain shows was on when we got there. In the middle of the pool with Apollo and his horses, water spurted high in the air, Rameau's music played, and for fifteen minutes, the air was filled with a cooling display around the pool statues. It was enchanting. We sat on one of the benches and cooled off just watching all that water shooting up toward the sky.

We thanked Annette for our tour, and Tina called Officer Paulhe on her cell. We walked back to the front of the palace, and our genial bodyguard was already there in his police van.

"You are through already?" he asked. "I thought you would stay for the fireworks and concert fountains tonight. It's amazing. You should really see it."

"Next time, Jacques," Gini said. "We need to get back to Paris."

I fell asleep in the van and didn't wake up until we were back on Boulevard du Montparnasse in front of the apartment.

"I will park and take my place outside your door," Officer Paulhe said. "I will keep you safe."

CANCANS, CROISSANTS, AND CASKETS

We were all tired from walking around in the heat all day, and after some bread and cheese, which we shared with our officer friend, we read for a while and then went to bed. Jacques sat in a chair outside our door, dozing on and off, throughout the night.

RECIPES FOR SOUFFLÉ ROLL, CRÊPES, AND SHRIMP SALAD

Soufflé Roll

Serves six.

Roll
4 tbsps. butter
½ cup flour
½ tsp. salt
⅛ tsp. white pepper
2 cups milk
5 eggs, separated

Filling
2 tbsps. butter
4 finely chopped shallots
4 chopped mushrooms
1 cup chopped cooked spinach
1 cup chopped cooked ham
1 tbsp. Dijon mustard
¼ tsp. nutmeg
2 3-ounce packages cream cheese
Salt and ground pepper

To make the roll
1. Preheat the oven to 400 degrees.
2. Grease a 15½ by 10½ by 1 inch jelly roll pan.
3. Line pan with greased waxed paper.

4. Dust waxed paper with flour.

5. Make a cream sauce: melt the butter in a saucepan; add flour, salt, and pepper; then slowly stir in the milk. Bring to a boil and cook for one minute.

6. Mix yolks, but don't overdo it.

7. Add yolks to cream sauce and heat one more minute. Don't let it boil, and keep stirring.

8. Let the mixture cool for a while.

9. Whip the egg whites until they are stiff, but don't let them get too dry.

10. Fold them into the cream sauce that is now room temperature.

11, Pour the mixture onto your greased, wax-papered jelly roll pan.

12. Bake for thirty minutes until the sheet of dough is puffy and brown. (Make the filling while the dough is baking)

13. Flip the whole thing onto a clean towel.

14. Fill the roll with the filling, and—this is the tricky part—using the towel to help you, roll it up and slide it onto a plate with the seam down. Cut up into six mouth-watering servings.

To make the filling

1. Sauté the shallots in the butter in a skillet until they are tender.

2. Add the mushrooms and cook them about three minutes. You want to get rid of their moisture.

3. Stir in the spinach, ham, mustard, and nutmeg, and heat.

4. Add the cream cheese, salt, and pepper.

5. Spread it on your beautifully browned, puffy roll.

Crêpes with Mushroom and Bacon

Makes 12 crêpes.

Crêpes
1 large egg
1 cup milk
1 tbsp. melted butter
1 tsp. chopped parsley
½ cup flour
½ tsp. salt
½ tsp. ground black pepper
Vegetable oil

Filling
6 slices bacon
1½ pound thinly sliced mushrooms
3 tbsps. butter
¼ cup flour
1 cup milk
½ cup heavy cream
1 tbsp. chopped parsley

To make the crêpes
1. Whisk together egg, milk, butter, and parsley.
2. Add flour, salt, and pepper.
3. Heat eight-inch crêpe pan until hot.
4. Heat oil in pan until hot.
5. Pour about ⅛ cup of batter into the pan, tilting the pan until the bottom is covered with

the batter. You want very thin crêpes, so don't pour too much batter into the pan.

6. When the crêpe is lightly browned on the bottom, turn it over with a spatula and brown the other side.

7. Keep making crêpes until you have used up all the batter—makes about twelve crêpes, maybe more.

To make the filling

1. Preheat oven to 200 degrees.

2. Cook bacon until crisp and drain on paper towels.

3. Chop the bacon.

4. Leave about 1 tbsp. of bacon fat in the skillet, and add 1 tbsp. of butter to it.

5. Sauté the mushrooms in the bacon fat and butter until they're done, about five minutes.

6. Make a roux by melting 2 tbsps. of butter in a heavy saucepan and whisking in the flour. Cook for three minutes, stirring the whole time.

7. Gradually add the milk, constantly whisking, until the roux is thick and smooth; should take five minutes or so.

8. Add the sautéed mushrooms, heavy cream, parsley, bacon, salt, and pepper, and simmer for ten minutes. It should be very thick.

9. Put about ¼ cup of filling in each crêpe and fold them over.

11. Each person gets two crêpes (or invite fewer people and serve each person more crêpes).

Shrimp, Orange, and Anchovy Salad

Serves four.

24 raw, unshelled medium-sized shrimp
6 ground allspice
Salt
2 small red-skin onions, peeled
4 seedless, peeled oranges
8 flat anchovy fillets
Kalamata olives, pitted

Sauce Vinaigrette with Rosemary
2 tsps. Dijon mustard
Salt and freshly ground pepper to taste
½ tsp. chopped garlic
4 tsps. red wine vinegar
½ cup corn oil
1 tsp. chopped fresh rosemary

To make the sauce vinaigrette
1. Put the mustard, garlic, salt and pepper, and vinegar in bowl.
2. Whisk in corn oil gradually until mixture thickens.
3. Stir in fresh rosemary.

To cook the shrimp and prepare the salad
1. Put shrimp, ground allspice, and salt in a saucepan, and just cover with cold water.
2. Bring to a boil.

3. Turn off heat. Let shrimp stand in water until it becomes room temperature.

4. Shell and devein shrimp.

5. Cut onions up into ¼-inch slices, put them in a bowl, and pour boiling water over them.

6. Stir onions for fifteen seconds, then drain and chill in ice water.

7. Slice oranges and arrange on four salad plates.

8. Place shrimp on oranges.

9. Put onion slices on top of shrimp.

10. Place two anchovies on top of each salad.

11. Dress salads with sauce vinaigrette.

12. Add Kalamata olives.

**Janice's Fashion Tip: Get a great haircut
to go with those summer dresses while
you're in Paris.**

Chapter 16

Want Some Raspberries to Go with That Frozen Lemon Soufflé?

Gini woke me early the next morning.
"Wake up, sleepyhead," she said. "I signed
us up for a cooking class this morning, and we
have to be there by eleven-thirty."

"Gini, I don't care about cooking," I said. "I
don't even care about eating. I'll just stay here
and read. The rest of you can go, but I'm not
going."

"I know you don't like to cook," Gini said.
"I'm not crazy about it either. But this is really
great. It's a dessert cooking class, and we get to
eat all the things we cook. I mean, think of it,

Jan. Tarte tatin. Frozen lemon soufflé. Napoleons. Nobody makes desserts like the French. You have to come."

Mary Louise, already dressed, poked her head in the door. "Come on, Jan," she said. "You need to get out of here and have some fun on our last day in Paris. We'll be with you. Officer Paulhe will be with us too. You can't spend your last day in Paris shut up in this apartment."

"They might even make my favorite," Pat said. Chocolate sou—oh, I mean a—uh—a chocolate mousse."

Even I had to laugh at Pat's gaffe. That's all I needed. One look at a chocolate soufflé and I'd be on the next plane home.

"I know this is tough, Jan," Tina said. "But you'll be glad you did it. Please come. We have more fun when you're with us."

Tina always knows exactly the right thing to say. How could I resist her?

"Well, OK," I said. "You talked me into it."

"You'll be so glad you did, Jan," Gini said. "The woman who teaches this class is brilliant. She teaches at the Cordon Bleu—you know, the most famous cooking school in the world, practically—and she knew Julia Child. She took one of her courses when she was very young. She's fun too. She teaches this class for tourists in her home, which is the most warm and welcoming place I've ever been in."

"But what about that poor police guy out there?" I said. "How will he feel about going to a cooking class?"

"He's French!" Gini said. "He'll probably love it. Beats looking for little pieces of glass in that club."

"Gini," Tina said, frowning, "maybe we could stay off that subject for a while."

"Oh, sorry, Jan," Gini said. "Sometimes I talk before I think."

"Sometimes?" Pat said. "How about every time you open your mouth?"

"I'm not the one who brought up the chocolate sou—"

"Case closed," Pat said. "Get dressed."

Cooking class. It wasn't my favorite way to spend part of my last day in Paris, but it wasn't the worst either. What the heck, it would take my mind off Anderson and Ahmet and chlorine gas.

We told Officer Paulhe where we were going, and his smile told us he was delighted to accompany us. "Très, très bien, mes petites," he said. "Allons-y." In other words. "Very good. Let's go."

Officer Paulhe hailed a cab, and we scrunched in the back while he sat up front with the driver. Gini told us later the cabbie congratulated the police officer for his arduous duty—having to guard five beautiful women. We drove to the Champs Élysées on the Right Bank and turned off onto a side street with very expensive-looking buildings, the kind we have on the Upper East Side in New York. You know just by looking at them that only rich people could afford to live there.

Tina paid the driver, and we were buzzed into the building. A voice told us to come to the fourth floor. An attractive woman in her seventies opened the door for us and ushered us into a sunlit living room, where a black King Charles spaniel welcomed us with barks and a wagging tail.

"Woofy," the lady said. "Hush."

"He loves company," she said, her accent charmingly French. "I am so glad to see you. I've seen your films, Gini. It's an honor to meet you."

"I've always wanted to do a documentary about you," Gini said. "We have to talk about that." She introduced each of us to the woman, whose name was Madame Arnaud.

"Come into my kitchen," she said.

Our gentle police officer looked uncertain as to whether he was included in this invitation. We could tell that he wanted to be part of this marvelous experience, but wasn't sure if he should follow us.

"Monsieur, venez," Madame Arnaud said. She took his arm and led him into her perfect kitchen. The rest of us followed. The room was huge and bright, with pots and pans hung on a rack above the counter where she would cook. There were colorful jars containing spatulas, wooden spoons, and knives, small bowls full of spices and liquids. Much as I hate cooking, I was seduced by this room.

"If you are ready," she said, "take your seats on the stools on the other side of the counter and we will begin. I will start with a tarte tatin. You will have a chance to participate as we go along. Do not worry. I will get us started.

"First, we make the pie crust. You are all pie makers chez vous?"

"We really only have one member of our group who cooks a lot, madame," Gini said. "Mary Louise Temple loves it. The rest of us are better eaters than cooks."

"Bon!" she said. "Mary Louise, you will be my assistant, and we will try to teach the others a little something as we go along. Ça va?"

"Ça va," Mary Louise said. Her beaming expression assured Madame she was her willing helper.

"The most important thing to remember when you make this pie crust," Madame said, "Is that you must use very cold butter and ice water so that your dough will be firm and easy to handle. Put a cup of flour, one-eighth teaspoon of salt, and one quarter cup of sugar through the sieve into a bowl. Then you add a quarter of a pound of butter—very cold butter, remember—

to the dry ingredients with a pastry blender. It should look like crumbs when you are finished. Then you add three tablespoons of ice water. You sprinkle it in like this and toss the pastry with a fork. Form it into a ball. You must use a very light touch when you do this. It's the difference between a heavy dough and a light one. You understand me so far? The light crust is crucial to a good tarte tatin."

We nodded, but I knew I would never be able to make my hands fly around that ball of dough the way she did.

"I will put this dough in waxed paper and refrigerate it while I do the next part," she said. "I will ask my assistant, Madame Temple, to do this part, if she would like."

Mary Louise bounded to the other side of the counter to stand next to Madame Arnaud.

"I like an enthusiastic helper," she said, smiling at Mary Louise. "This next part is very easy. Please grease this pie plate with two tablespoons of butter, and sprinkle on three tablespoons of sugar. You need a deep nine-inch pie plate for this tarte."

Mary Louise did us proud, expertly smearing the butter all over the bottom of the pie plate.

"Excellent," Madame said. "Now please sprinkle three tablespoons of sugar over the butter. Très bien. Next, you will arrange these three red delicious apples, which I have peeled and sliced neatly, in layers over the butter and sugar."

As if she did this every day of her life, Mary Louise placed the apples in the pie plate.

"You must stay in Paris and be my assistant every day," Madame said.

"If only I could," Mary Louise said. "This is so much fun."

"Next, my little assistant, please take the rest of the butter—four tablespoons are left—and dot the apples with them. You understand 'dot'?"

"Like this?" Mary Louise asked as she used a knife to take small pats of butter and plunk them on the apples.

"Perfect," Madame said. "Now, sprinkle three tablespoons of sugar over the butter and apples and you are finished—for now."

Mary Louise sprinkled the sugar and stepped back.

Madame took the ball of dough out of the refrigerator. "Next I will roll out this pie dough until it is just the right size to fit over the apples."

"I always have trouble with this," Mary Louise said. "Lots of times the dough tears, and I can't get it in one neat round."

"It does not matter if it tears," Madame said. "Dough will do that. You just have a little bowl of water near you and dip your finger in it and mend the tear in the dough with that. It won't show when the crust is baked."

It was a pleasure, even for me, the non-cook,

to watch her place the dough on a floured surface, and quickly, expertly, with the least amount of pressure and effort, roll out the dough to a perfect nine-inch layer to place over the apples. She had no tears to mend.

"I have heated the oven to 375 degrees," she said, "And we will cook this for thirty minutes. While it is cooking, I will show you how to make a frozen lemon soufflé."

I felt my friends stiffen at the word *soufflé*, but I was all right since it wasn't preceded by the word *chocolate*.

"This is my favorite dessert after a three-course dinner," she said. "It's the perfect way to end a meal. Light and delicious."

She gave Mary Louise a little hug and said, "You are the perfect assistant, ma chère, but we must give your friends a chance to participate also."

She beckoned to Tina. "Would you like to help, madame?"

Tina jumped up and took Mary Louise's place behind the counter.

"With pleasure," she said. "I'm not as good a cook as my friend, but I do like to try new things. I'm Tina Powell."

Madame Arnaud brought out a one-quart soufflé dish and handed Tina a piece of waxed paper with butter spread on it.

"This will not test your cooking, just your

wrapping skill, Madame Powell," she said. She handed Tina some string and told her to wrap the waxed paper all the way around the top sides of the soufflé dish so that it stood up about three inches above the dish.

"Why is she doing that?" Gini asked. If something doesn't seem logical to Gini, she always asks.

"Because," Madame answered, "The soufflé will rise above the top of the dish, and this waxed paper will keep it from falling out. Vous comprenez?"

"Oui, je comprends," Gini said, always glad to speak French. "I understand."

"While Madame Powell is doing that, I will put one tablespoon of gelatin in a quarter of a cup of cold water and let it soften. While it is sitting there, I will separate six eggs. Do any of you know how to do that?"

Mary Louise raised her hand timidly. "I can do it, but I always make a mess," she said. "Could I watch you do it?"

"But of course," Madame said. "I have done it so often, it's easy for me, but I understand it can be messy. Watch and I will show you how."

She brought out three bowls and six eggs. "The tricky part is that this recipe calls for six egg yolks, but only four egg whites, so I must put two of the separated egg whites into this small bowl to save for another time or perhaps to make an egg-white omelet tomorrow morning."

She cracked each of the six eggs on the side of the bowl, and without allowing one speck of yolk to get into the egg whites, she smoothly, without any mess, separated the eggs into yolks and whites.

"It's very important not to let any yolk get into the whites because then you cannot beat the whites properly," she said. "Now, who would like to beat these egg yolks with a cup of sugar?"

"I can do that," Tina said. She had tied the waxed paper around the soufflé dish so that it looked presentable. Madame poured the egg yolks into a saucepan and gave Tina the sugar and a wire whisk. "They must be very light and very thick," she said. "Beat them strenuously."

Tina lit into those egg yolks with a vengeance until they passed Madame's test. "Excellent," she said. "Now we stir two-thirds of a cup of lemon juice into that." She looked at us sternly. "*Not* that excuse for lemon juice that comes in bottles, but lemon juice from real lemons. That is very important."

I felt as if I had committed some crime since I always used bottled lemon juice. I didn't even own a lemon squeezer. And there were all those pits that kept falling in the juice.

Tina, who probably used bottled lemon juice too, added the real stuff to her concoction of yolks and sugar and stirred it in. Madame nodded her approval. "Very good. Now you will cook this over a low flame, beating it the whole time until it is very thick. But do not," again she looked stern, "do not let it boil. That would totally ruin it."

Tina looked a little nervous. "Maybe you'd better do that part, Madame," she said. "I'd hate to do it wrong."

Madame's expression softened. "Oh, do not worry, chérie," she said. "I would not let you ruin it, but if you wish, I will finish this part."

Tina looked immensely relieved. "If you don't mind, Madame," she said and came back to our side of the counter.

Madame started to beat the mixture in the saucepan, when she looked up and noticed our police officer watching eagerly on his stool next to us. He obviously wanted to be a part of this but was too timid to volunteer. Madame took pity on him.

"We need a strong arm for this," she said. "Perhaps, monsieur, you will help us?"

Office Paulhe was off his seat and behind the counter before she could finish her sentence. He started beating the mixture, and his whole face showed how much he was enjoying this.

"You have done this before, monsieur?" Madame asked.

"Oui, Madame," he said, not stopping, "Cooking is a great pleasure for me."

When he had achieved just the right consistency, Madame Arnaud said, "Now you may add the gelatin and one tablespoon of grated lemon rind. Another reason not to use bottled juice. It has no rinds."

We laughed politely.

"Next, monsieur, perhaps you would like to use this hand mixer to beat the four egg whites until they are stiff, but not too dry."

He nodded eagerly and turned on the mixer.

"While our chef is doing that, perhaps one of you will whip this heavy cream with the other mixer until it is firm," Madame said.

We all sat there, not moving, until Gini stood up and went around the counter. "How hard could it be?" she said. "I'll do that."

"Brave woman," Madame said, handing her the bowl of cream.

Soon the noise of electric mixers filled the air. I was getting hungrier and hungrier. I assumed we would get to taste this divine dessert when they finished their beating and whipping and stirring and mixing.

I tried not to think about last night and Alan Anderson, but bits and pieces of my ordeal kept creeping back into my mind. My friends were keeping a protective eye on me. When they noticed my face change, one or the other would take my hand or put an arm around my shoulder for a minute or say something to bring me back.

"Think Gini will beat that cream until it begs for mercy?" Mary Louise asked me.

I relaxed. "Probably," I said.

"Don't you love that police officer?" Tina said. "Can you imagine a New York police officer doing that?"

"Not really," I said, my mind back in the kitchen.

When the egg whites and the cream were just right, Madame took the mixers and thanked her helpers, who returned to their seats.

"Now we are coming to the best part. I will fold the eggs whites into our mixture, which has now cooled. And then I'll fold in the whipped cream. Do any of you know what I mean by 'fold'?"

Mary Louise and Officer Paulhe raised their hands. Madame said, "Madame Temple, tell us."

"You take a rubber spatula and sort of cut down through the cream and then fold it back up through the lemon mixture. You turn the bowl a little bit and repeat cutting and folding and turning the bowl until the whipped cream or the egg whites are thoroughly mixed in."

"Very good," Madame said. "I would only add that you want to do this very gently to preserve the delicacy of the frozen soufflé."

She did just that, first folding in the egg whites and then the whipped cream. When it was perfectly blended, she poured it into the soufflé dish with its waxed paper collar. There was too much of this confection to fit into the bowl, so the rest was held in place by the waxed paper. She smoothed the top of the mixture, said, "Voilà!" and put the dish in the freezer.

"It takes a while to freeze," she said. "But I made another one before you came and will let you taste it soon."

My whole being thanked her for this.

"To finish up our cooking lesson today," Madame said, "we will take our tarte tatin out of the oven and see if we did a good job."

We applauded, the police officer loudest of all.

"I'd better do this last part," Madame said, "because it's a little tricky."

She took the pie out of the oven and very carefully turned it upside down onto a large pan. The pie crust was on the bottom and the apples were now on top. She sprinkled sugar all over the top of this mouth-watering delight and slipped it under the broiler for a brief time until the sugar turned a luscious light brown.

When it came out of the oven, it was the most beautiful thing I had ever seen. I was so hungry by this time that I would have eaten it with my fingers, but Madame had set a table in another part of the kitchen with a rose linen cloth and pale pink roses in bowls in the center. She told us to sit wherever we wanted, and then she put a square of the tarte in front of each of us.

One taste and I was transported into some kind of pie heaven. Just the right balance of sweetness and tartness. A crust that was so light I barely had to chew it. I knew I could never make this at home, but I planned to encourage Mary Louise to cook it as soon as we got back to New Jersey. She read my mind.

"Can't wait till I try this at home," she said.

"Me too," I said. "As soon as possible."

"Madame," Mary Louise said, "could you please give us the recipes for the tarte tatin and the lemon soufflé?"

"Of course, my dear," she said. "That's part of this class. I have them all written out for you to take with you."

We were still savoring every bite of the tatin, when Madame went to the fridge and brought out a previously made frozen lemon soufflé. She sprinkled the top with fresh raspberries and spooned out portions for each of us.

It was a perfect counterpart to the warm tarte tatin. The cold and infinitely delicious, lighter-than-light, frozen lemon soufflé left us speechless. With our group that's a small miracle.

Finally, Gini looked around the table at all our happy faces and said, "Madame, we will remember you forever. Thank you for this feast."

"You are delightful," she said. "I must come and see you dance. How long will you be on the Bateau Mouche?"

"Unfortunately," Tina said, "the rest of our performances have been canceled because of— um—a couple of disastrous occurrences."

"She means a couple of murders, Madame Arnaud," Gini said.

"I read about them," she said. "I didn't know you were involved. Do they know who did it?"

"We have a pretty good idea," Gini said, "But they need proof."

"Well, I'm sorry I won't get to see you," Madame said. "If anything changes and you do dance again before you leave, will you let me know?"

"Of course we will," Tina said. "Thank you again for today, Madame. We'd better be on our way."

Madame's little black spaniel sat patiently nearby.

"What a good dog," Pat said.

"He's well trained," Madame said. "He knows he can't beg for food when I have guests." She held out a piece of tarte tatin for him to taste, and he gobbled it up in seconds.

"Is he called 'Woofy' because he woofs?" I asked.

"No, actually, his real name is Wolfgang Amadeus Mozart," she said. "Woofy, for short. I love Mozart's music."

We all leaned down for a last pat to Woofy's soft head as we left the apartment with Officer Paulhe. Madame handed Mary Louise the recipes as she left.

RECIPES FOR TARTE TATIN AND FROZEN LEMON SOUFFLÉ

Tarte Tatin

Pie Crust
1 cup flour
⅛ tsp. salt
¼ cup sugar
¼ lb. butter
3 tbsps. ice water

Filling
6 tbsps. butter
½ cup sugar
3 cup peeled, sliced Red Delicious apples

To make the crust
1. Preheat the oven to 375 degrees.
2. Sift the flour, salt, and sugar into a bowl.
3. Add the butter with a pastry blender.
4. Add the ice water and form mixture into a ball.
5. Roll out the pastry to make a nine-inch circle.
6. Grease a deep nine-inch pie tin with three tbsps. of the butter.
7. Sprinkle three tbsps. of sugar over the butter in the pie tin.
8. Put the apples in layers over the butter and sugar.

9. Dot the apples with four tbsps. of butter.

10. Sprinkle three tbsps. of sugar on top of the butter and apples.

11. Cover the apples with the nine-inch pie crust.

12. Bake for thirty minutes.

13. Turn off the oven. Turn on the broiler.

14. Turn the pie tin upside down over a broiler pan very carefully. The pie crust will now be on the bottom and the apples on top.

15. Sprinkle apples with whatever sugar is left.

16. Put the pan under the broiler just briefly, until the sugar is brown.

Mary McHugh

Frozen Lemon Soufflé

1 tbsp. gelatin
¼ cup cold water
6 egg yolks
1 cup sugar
⅔ cup lemon juice (squeezed from lemons, not from a bottle)
1 tbsp. grated lemon rind
4 egg whites
1½ cups heavy cream
1 cup fresh raspberries

1. Take a 1-quart soufflé dish and tie buttered waxed paper around it so that it extends three inches above the soufflé dish.

2. Put the gelatin in the water to soften it.

3. Put the egg yolks and sugar in a saucepan and beat them until they are very thick and light. Add the lemon juice.

4. Keep beating them over a low flame, without letting them boil, until they are thick.

5. Stir in the gelatin until it dissolves.

6. Add the lemon rind.

7. Cool the mixture.

8. Beat the egg whites and fold into the cooled mixture.

9. Whip the heavy cream and fold that in.

10. Pour the mixture into the soufflé dish. The waxed paper will hold the part that rises above the dish.

11. Freeze the soufflé until it's set.
12. Peel off the waxed paper
13 Sprinkle the fresh raspberries on top of the soufflé.
14. Enjoy!

Janice's Fashion Tip: Yes, you will need an umbrella for those sudden summer showers in Paris.

Chapter 17

Parlez-Vous Français?

"Thanks, guys," I said when we were outside. "I feel much better. That was great. Now what?"

"Mesdames," our sweet police officer said, "I'm afraid our next stop won't be as good as this one."

Uh-oh, I thought. *What terrible thing does he have in mind?* This was not like me at all. I'm usually up for anything that comes along, but that was before I was almost killed. That tends to make you a little nervous for a while.

"What's happening, Officer Paulhe?" Tina asked.

"Captain Chantal just texted me," he said. "We are to return to the bateau to meet her there with the rest of the band and Suzette. She's sending a car here to meet us."

"Is Alan Anderson going to be there?" I asked. "I don't want to go anywhere if he's there."

"La capitaine didn't mention him," the officer said. "But you must not worry, madame. I will not let anything happen to you."

I was so grateful to this officer I wanted to give him a big kiss on the cheek, but I knew that wouldn't be appropriate. "Merci, Monsieur Paulhe," I said.

"Ah, you are beginning to speak French," he said, smiling at me.

"I wish," I said. "Gini, maybe you could teach us a little Frenchbefore we leave. You know, just simple phrases that we can use the next time we come to Paris."

"Of course, Jan," she said. "That's 'bien sûr' in French. I'll try to remember to do that. It's such a beautiful language. I'm glad you want to learn it."

"At least the basics, Gini," Pat said.

"I think you have a very willing teacher already," Gini said, grinning at Pat.

"If you mean Geneviève," Pat said, "she speaks perfect English."

"Just saying," Gini said. "You know, useful phrases, like 'Je t'aime.' "

"Knock it off, Gini," Pat said. "I told you it's

not like that with us. We don't say 'I love you' to each other in English or French."

"Not yet anyway," Gini said.

"Leave her alone, Gini," Tina said. Gini never knows when to stop.

"Ah, voilà," said Officer Paulhe.

A police van pulled up next to us and we piled in. Officer Paulhe sat in front with the driver.

"To the bateau," he said.

Fifteen minutes later we were at the pier. We could see Captain Chantal waiting for us on the boat. My stomach was doing flip-flops as I followed my friends up the ramp. Our guardian officer was right behind me.

The band and Suzette were in their usual places at the front of the vessel. Ken waved hello to me as we joined them. Suzette looked startled when she saw us, but quickly regained her composure and nodded without smiling. Her shih tzu yipped when he saw us. She popped some kind of doggy treat into his mouth.

"I am sorry to disrupt your day," the captain said, "but Jean asked me to bring you here. Go ahead, Jean. Explain your problem to our American friends."

"I must ask a great favor of you," he said to us. "Nobody canceled the program for tonight. I thought somebody else had called it off, but it seems a large crowd of Americans booked our bateau to celebrate a birthday of one their group—her sixtieth birthday. She asked especially for our band and Suzette and for you. We couldn't disappoint her. Could you possibly dance tonight? I know it's short notice and I . . ."

"Of course we will, Jean," Tina said. "We were supposed to dance on this boat all week, so we will certainly be here."

Jean's face reflected his relief. "Thank you, Tina," he said. "What would you like to dance to tonight?"

"Do you know 'Pigalle'?" Tina asked.

"Mais oui! Bien sûr," Jean said. "It's one of our favorites. And Suzette loves it, n'est-ce pas, Suzette?"

"Comment?" she said, not looking at him. "Quoi?" She was clearly annoyed.

" 'Pigalle,' " Jean repeated. "Is it okay if we do that song tonight?"

"I don't care what you do," Suzette said, turning her back on us and starting to speak to Claude in French.

"What's wrong with Suzette?" Gini asked.

"She's bummed," Jean said. "She thought she was leaving for New York tomorrow, and now it looks as if she won't be able to."

"Why not? Gini asked.

"I'm not sure," Jean answered. "Something about Anderson being delayed, I think."

At the mention of Anderson, I felt nauseous. I sat down. My friends gathered around me.

"Are you all right, Jan?" Mary Louise asked. "You don't look good."

"Give me a minute," I said.

Jean came over to me. He looked concerned.

"Qu'est-ce qu'il y a, ma petite?" he asked me. I assumed he was asking me what the matter was. I particularly liked his calling me petite.

"Jean," I said, "will Anderson be here tonight when we perform?

"I'm not sure," Jean said. "I'm never sure with him. Why? Did you want to see him?"

"No, I'd rather not see him," I said.

Captain Chantal put her hand on my shoulder. "I'll make sure he's not here, Janice," she said. "We're still investigating him."

"You're investigating Anderson?" Jean asked. "Why?"

"We don't know if he has proper clearance to take Suzette out of the country," the captain said. "Until we are sure, they cannot leave Paris."

Suzette turned away from Claude abruptly and exploded in a rapid stream of French at Captain Chantal. Her face was tense and angry, her gestures threatening. I assumed she was protesting the captain's decision.

Geneviève answered her quietly but intensely. There was no mistaking her attitude: I'll decide when you can leave the country. Don't mess with me, honey.

Pierrot, the little shih tzu, jumped out of Suzette's grasp and skittered around, barking at the police captain as loudly as his tiny body could manage, yapping and yipping, defending his mistress with all his might.

He broke the tension. It was hard to stay angry watching this fierce little puppy.

Suzette picked up her tiny dog and soothed him. "Ça va, Pierrot," she said. "Shhh." She kissed the top of his head, and he burrowed into her shoulder.

Suzette straightened up and said to Tina, "Alors, ma chère, shall we rehearse our number for tonight?" She wasn't smiling.

"Good idea," Tina said. "Let's do a quick run-through of 'Pigalle,' just to be sure we get the right tempo and all. OK with you, Jean?"

"Fine with me," Jean said.

Tina alerted all of us while Jean got his band ready to perform, and Suzette put a bowl of food on the floor for Pierrot.

I love this song. Again, it reminds me of my honeymoon in Paris with Derek because we really liked the section of the city called Pigalle. It's in Montmartre, and is raunchy and not too safe. The touristy nightclub Moulin Rouge is there in all its flashy glory, featuring topless dancers and lots of skirt-swirling cancans.

We lined up at the front of the stage. When the band started the fast and joyful strains of the song, Jean blasting away on his horn, Yves actually awake and drumming, Claude plunking his cello, and my friend Ken playing fast and furiously on the keyboard, we swung into our dance with a vengeance. While Suzette sang of sidewalk cafés, taxi's horns, naughty ladies working the streets where rich and poor come together, we danced our version of the cancan, backs turned to the audience, skirts lifted up to tease, flashing knees and sparkling, moving feet, never stopping, always promising things we had no intention of delivering, faster and faster until the last line of the song urging visitors to Paree not to miss Pigalle.

We were breathing hard as we finished and collapsed in chairs nearby as the band and Suzette finished.

"That was great," Jean said, out of breath himself as he congratulated us. "Should go really well tonight."

"Thanks Jean," Tina said. "I'm glad we tried it out first. You played the exact beat we wanted. You're really good. What time do you want us here tonight?"

"Come about seven and you'll perform at eight-thirty. OK?"

"Perfect," Tina said. "See you at seven."

Officer Paulhe—though we all called him Jacques now—appeared, beaming at us as if we were his own sisters. "Magnifique," he said to us.

We followed him off the boat to the police van that would take us back to the apartment.

While Jacques stood guard outside our door, we scrounged around in the fridge to find some food to sustain us until the performance that evening. I didn't really need much. I was still full from our tarte tatin and frozen soufflé, but I needed a little something to get me through our strenuous dance coming up.

There was some cheese—brie and chèvre—a couple of loaves of French bread that weren't too stale, a bottle of chardonnay, and some chicken liver paté. My idea of a feast, actually.

We spread it all out on our table and gathered around it to munch and sip and talk about our Paris adventure.

"How are you doing, Jan?" Tina asked. "Are you OK for tonight and one more day here? If you have any qualms at all about staying, I'll cancel tomorrow and we'll fly back in the morning."

"I think I'm all right, Tina," I said, in between bites of the chèvre and paté. "I feel safe with our nice police officer out there guarding me. I don't see how Anderson or Ahmet can get at me again with him there."

"Geneviève promised me she wouldn't let anything happen to you," Pat said. "I believe her. She's really good at her job."

"I'd feel better if she could find some clue, some evidence, of my experience last night," I said. "Otherwise, they have no reason to arrest Alan. I won't have that police guy out there with me forever. Alan or Ahmet could get rid of me back in New York."

"She'll find something," Pat said. "Don't worry, Jan. She's extremely thorough, and she has her whole staff working on it."

"Do you think Suzette knows anything about the murders of Monsieur and Madame Fouchet?" Gini asked. "I get the feeling that she'd do anything to get to New York."

"I don't see how she could possibly not know something about them," Gini said. "It seems way too convenient that the two people keeping her from leaving the bateau and going to New York with Anderson are now dead."

"She sure lit into Geneviève this afternoon," Mary Louise said. "I don't understand French, but it was clear that she objected violently to the captain's order to keep her here in Paris."

"Speaking of not understanding French," Gini said, "do you guys want a quick French lesson in useful phrases?"

"Yes, yes, and yes again," I said, and the rest of my hoofing friends chimed in with their own yeses. "Start off with that 'n'est-ce pas' thing they're always sticking in at the end of a sentence. What is that?"

"It just means 'isn't that so?' " Gini said. "Sort of like our 'right?' "

"Does 'quoi?' just mean 'what?' " Tina asked.

"Exactly," Gini said. "But let me tell you some really useful things to say. Even if you don't get the accent exactly right, the French will give you credit for trying. They're proud that their accent is so difficult—especially their *r*'s, which you have to pronounce as if you're going to hawk something out of your throat but then change your mind. Don't worry about it."

"So how do you say, 'What is your name?' " Mary Louise asked. "I always like to know a person's name."

"You say, 'Comment vous appelez vous?' " Gini said, "Which literally means, 'How do you call yourself?' And if someone asks you what your name is, you say, 'Je m'appelle Mary Louise,' which you can probably figure out means 'I call myself Mary Louise.' "

"I have one for you," Tina said. "I know 'au revoir' is 'good-bye,' but I've heard you say 'à bientôt' sometimes when you're leaving. What does that mean?"

"It's just 'see you soon,' " Gini said. "It's more informal, a little friendlier than 'au revoir,' which means literally 'until the next time I see you.' "

"Suppose you want to thank somebody more than just 'merci,' " I asked. "I mean, you really, really want to say thanks."

"Then you say 'merci mille fois,' which is 'thank you a thousand times," Gini said.

"I have another one for you," I said. "How do I say, 'Where is the nearest place to get my hair cut?' I don't want to go home without a French haircut."

"You say, 'Ou est le salon de beauté le plus

proche?' " Gini said, "which means, 'Where is the closest beauty salon?' Why don't you practice by asking our friend Jacques that question. He probably knows where everything is around here."

"Great idea," I said, and put down my chèvre and bread to go to the door and open it.

No Jacques in sight. *Uh-oh*, I thought. *This is not good.*

I quickly closed the door and said, "He's not there. I'm scared."

"Don't panic," Pat said. "I'll call Geneviève. He probably just went to get something to eat at the Select across the street. He can watch everyone coming into the building from there."

"Please call her, Pat," I said.

Pat dialed a number on her cell phone. She waited. "Got her voice mail," she said to us and then, "Geneviève, it's Pat. Please call me as soon as possible."

"We're not going anywhere until one of them turns up, Jan," Tina said. "Don't worry." She looked at her watch. "In the meantime, we'd better get dressed. It's five-thirty. Who's first in the shower?"

"I'll go," Gini said. "I'm the fastest." She headed for the shower.

Mary Louise gathered up the remaining cheese, bread, and wine and put them back in the fridge, then sponged off the table until it was shiny clean.

"Next," Gini said, running past us in a towel. "What are we wearing, Tina?"

"Our slutty red-and-white cancan dresses," she said. "The ones with almost no tops and ruffled skirts we can flip up. Black net stockings. Our sexiest high heels."

Mary Louise disappeared into the shower room. I opened the apartment door again to see if my friend Jacques had reappeared.

No one was outside our door. I couldn't believe Jacques would desert us like that. Just disappear without telling us where he was going. I felt so safe when he was there. I stepped out into the hallway to see if he was on his way up in the elevator. The door closed behind me, and a hand covered my mouth. A dark-skinned hand. To my right I could see a body lying on the floor. A body in a police uniform. Jacques. I felt something pressing into my back.

"Do not make a sound or you're dead," he said. He had an Indian accent. I knew it was Ahmet.

"Walk very carefully down the staircase," he said. "Try to get away and I'll shoot you. I mean it. Do exactly as I say and you'll be all right. Do you understand?"

I nodded. I had no intention of arguing with a gun. I held tightly to the railing next to the stairs. I felt like I could fall at any minute.

When we got to the ground floor, he opened a door into a hallway I had not seen before. At the end of the long hallway was another door, which he opened, shoving me inside a small room with a couple of chairs, a table, and a bed.

"Remember, not a sound," he said, pushing me into a chair and pointing the gun at me.

"Where are we?" I asked

"No one knows about this room," he said. "A long time ago, there was a concierge who lived here, but they haven't had a concierge for years. No one will think of looking for you here. Not even the police."

The concierge? I thought. *No one knows about this room? There's one person who does.*

"How did you know about it?" I asked.

"I made it my business to look through every part of this building before I grabbed you," he said. "I knew I couldn't take you outside because they would be searching for me when you turned up missing. I stumbled upon this room by accident and knew no one would think of looking here."

There has to be a way, I thought. *Think, Jan, think.*

"What do you want from me?" I asked.

"It's simple," he said. "I will call the police captain—what's her name—Chantal. I will tell her that I am holding you prisoner and that she must allow Monsieur Anderson and Mademoiselle Suzette to get on a plane to New York today or I will kill you. To prove that I am telling the truth, I will hand you the phone. You must tell her that I am not lying and she must do as I ask. That's all you will say. If you try to tell her anything else, those will be the last words you speak." He brought the gun closer to me.

"I'll do whatever you say," I said. "Call her."

Ahmet dialed her direct line. When she picked up, he said, "Captain Chantal? Please listen carefully to what I have to say. I am holding Madame Janice Rogers, one of the dancers, hostage. If you want to see her alive again, you will see that Monsieur Anderson and Mademoiselle Suzette are on the next plane to New York. I will release her when I hear from him in New York, that he has not been arrested. Do not be mistaken, ma capitaine, I will kill Madame Rogers without any hesitation if you do not do as I say."

He listened to her for a moment and then handed his phone to me. "She wants to hear your voice. Just tell her I'm telling the truth." He put the gun to my head. "Remember—nothing else."

"Hello, Genève," I said. I emphasized the name. "He is telling you the truth. Believe me, Genève. Do as he says."

There was a brief pause. "Understood," she said. I handed the phone back to Ahmet. He hung up.

"Stay where you are," he said. "We'll be in this room until I hear from Monsieur Anderson that he is safely off the plane in New York. That could be a long time. Don't try anything funny."

"How did you get involved in this whole thing?" I asked him. I wanted to get him talking without the gun in his hand.

"Very simple. Monsieur Anderson paid me a great deal of money to kill Monsieur and Madame Fouchet. I can go back to India and live in luxury for the rest of my life. I'd be there now if you hadn't mentioned that stupid earring."

"Did you put something in my drink to make me pass out at the club?" I asked.

"Not in your drink. In the shrimp bisque. I put some knock-out drops in the soup. I knew you wouldn't taste them because the bisque has such a strong flavor. My idea." He actually looked proud of his ingenuity. He put the gun on the table beside his chair. It was not near enough for me to grab.

"How did you get the chlorine gas into that room?"

"That was easy. Through the air-conditioning vents. We attached hoses to the gas and pulled them through the vents into your room."

"How come you have chlorine gas lying around like that?"

"We use chlorine as a pesticide and as a water purifier. There are lots of uses for it. We turned it into a gas and piped it into your room."

"What did you seal the door and windows with?"

"It's just an ordinary sealant people use in their homes when they don't have storm windows. These are old doors and windows that are very drafty, so we always have a supply of the sealant to use. It only took a couple of minutes to do it, and we thought you wouldn't wake up until the gas had killed you. The only thing we forgot was the door going into the bathroom. We thought we could leave that because we had sealed the bathroom window. Big mistake."

"How did you get everything cleaned up so quickly before the police got there?"

"I went outside to put some food in the Dumpster and noticed the broken glass under your window. It was obvious that you had landed in the Dumpster and gotten away. We tried to find you, but you must have already reached your apartment. We ripped off the sealant from the door and windows, used an industrial fan to get rid of the chlorine smell, and replaced the glass in less than an hour. We got rid of the Dumpster. Everything was back the way it was before the police arrived."

"Amazing," I said. I closed my eyes. "Do you mind if I sleep a little? I'm exhausted."

"Go ahead," he said. "I'll check my phone to see if anyone is trying to reach me."

I pretended to go to sleep, but sneaked a look

every now and then to make sure he didn't have the gun in his hand. Just the phone. My heart was in my mouth. Did Captain Chantal understand my message? She was very smart, but was that small clue of Catherine's special name for her enough to tell her where I was?

The police burst into the room so suddenly and quickly, Ahmet didn't have a chance to go for his gun. I dove for the floor, but they had him handcuffed and out the door before he could react.

Captain Chantal ran to help me up, and I collapsed into her arms. I was sobbing with relief.

"Oh, thank God, thank God," I said. "You got it. You knew. Oh, thank God."

"That was very clever of you, my dear Janice," she said, patting my back. "When you called me Genève, I knew exactly where you were. It's the only place in the world where anyone ever called me by that name. You were brilliant to remember that."

"Funny how brilliant you can be with a gun pressed to your head," I said. "But you were a genius to pick up on that name and come to get me."

Geneviève looked around this room that held so many memories for her. "It still feels the same in here," she said. "Small and cozy and private." For a moment she was fifteen again, alone with Catherine. She came back to the present and said to me, "Okay. Let me take you back to the apartment, where your friends are going out of their minds worrying about you."

"I'm supposed to dance on the bateau tonight," I said. "I'm not sure I can walk, let alone dance."

"No, no, there won't be a performance tonight," the captain said. "I canceled that after I sent my men to arrest Anderson and Suzette. They're safely in jail. Don't worry. Jean gave everybody their money back. That lady will just have to celebrate her birthday somewhere else."

"Officer Paulhe," I said. "Jacques. That nice man. Is he all right? He looked like he was dead. I saw him on the floor outside our apartment."

"He was unconscious. He's all right now, except that he feels like it was all his fault that you were captured. He'll be so glad to see you."

"It certainly wasn't his fault," I said. "I'll tell him. Thank goodness he's all right. We really like him. Did Suzette know about all this?"

"She's up to her ears in this whole thing," Geneviève said. "She wanted to go to New York so much that she went along with anything that had to be done to get there, including killing both Monsieur and Madame Fouchet."

"Did she know they tried to kill me?"

"I'm pretty sure she did. Anderson told her everything he was doing so she couldn't turn on him at any time. Even if she didn't actually help him kill them, she knew about it and can testify against him in court."

"Let's go back to the apartment," I said. "I need my friends."

Geneviève put her arm around me and helped me to the police car.

Chapter 18

Marlon Brando Ate Here

With a great rush of hugs and "Are you all right?" and "We were so worried," and lots of tears, my friends scooped me up and welcomed me back to the apartment. Geneviève made sure I was safe, told my sister Hoofers that we would not be dancing that night, and said she had to return to headquarters. Officer Paulhe was hovering nearby, a worried look on his face.

"Oh, Janeese," he said. "I will never forgive myself. I am so sorry."

I had to give him a hug. The poor man. "It wasn't your fault, Jacques. Are you all right? I thought you were dead when I saw you lying there."

"Do not worry, chérie," he said. "Just a bump on the head."

"I'll never forget you, my brave Jacques," I said to him.

He kissed me on the forehead and left the apartment. Geneviève started to follow him. I shook hands with her.

"À bientôt, Genève," I said. "Merci mille fois." Thanks to Gini I was practically fluent in French.

"I wish I could tell Catherine that her special name for me saved your life," the captain said.

"If it's all right with you, it will always be my special name for you too."

Geneviève smiled at me. "I think you earned the right to call me that," she said. "À bientôt, Janeese."

"À bientôt, Genève," I said, tears in my eyes.

She reached over to Pat and touched her hair. It was a tender gesture. "Perhaps we will meet again someday," she said. "You're a very special person."

Pat put her hand over Geneviève's. "You have to come to New York," she said. "I'll show you my city. Thank you for everything."

They shook hands and Geneviève left.

After she was gone, my friends made me tell them the whole story of Ahmet, the concierge's room, and my coded message to the captain.

"Incredible," Pat said. "If someone were pointing a gun at me, I wouldn't remember my own name, much less someone's secret name from long ago."

"Believe me, you'd remember," I said. "You'd remember everything anyone said to you from the time you were born. The instinct to survive, to stay alive, must be the strongest instinct we have."

Pat laughed. "You'll never believe this," she said, "but I wrote my doctoral thesis on the part that instincts play in our decisions and reactions. Wish I'd had this example to prove my point that we ignore our instincts at our peril."

"My instincts tell me that I'm starving and that we should go to one of the most famous restaurants of all times to celebrate Jan's rescue and our last night in Paris," Gini said.

"Ohhh, Gini," I said. "I can't move. I'm still in shock. Let's just stay here and eat some more bread and cheese. And a bunch of wine."

"Listen, Jan," she said. "We're only a couple of blocks away from La Coupole, Hemingway's restaurant. Great food, great atmosphere. We can't leave Paris without going there."

"I always thought that was just a touristy place," Pat said.

"Who cares?" Gini said. "It's still one of the best places to eat in the whole world. Come on, guys, we've got to have a blast our last night here."

They all looked at me. "It's up to you, Jan," Tina said. "If you aren't up to it, we'll stay here with you and eat some brie and bread."

The look on all their faces made me smile. How could I disappoint these women who would stay indoors on a warm summer's night in Paris to eat cheese and stale bread instead of going to one of the world's great restaurants just because they loved me?

"La Coupole it is," I said. "Let me get out of these sweaty clothes and I'll be right with you."

I changed into one of my favorite dresses—a blue-and-white silky number with a pleated, swirly skirt and my stiletto heels, which the police had returned to me.

"To La Coupole," I said. "How do you say, 'Let's go' in French, Gini?"

"Allons-y," she said.

We crowded into the elevator and went down to the ground floor.

I had a moment's shiver of horror when I saw the door leading to the hallway to the hidden concierge's room, but my friends swooped me out into the Paris night, and I was almost all right again.

There it was. The legendary La Coupole. The brasserie where Hemingway drank after writing all day. Where Josephine Baker could come in for dinner, accompanied by her leopard Chiquita, without being told the restaurant was for whites only. The place where you could see Picasso regaling his friends after a day of changing art forever. You might have been there the night Marlon Brando took off his shoes and ate barefoot. If you were really old, you might have dined at La Coupole when there was still a basin of water in the center of the restaurant where Kiki, the famous model, bathed naked.

We walked into this vast art deco palace, the dome overhead repainted recently in exuberant colors to reflect nature, celebration, and women, paintings on every wall, decorated fake marble columns, acres of tables covered in white linen, with flowers and silverware, waiting for the crowds of customers who came to this place every night to bask in the memories of Paris.

The maître d' ushered us to a large table on the side where we could see everything that was going on. I was so glad my friends had talked me into this. I wouldn't have missed it for the world.

The waiter greeted us and asked if we would like French or English menus. Gini asked for a French one, of course, and the rest of us copped out and took English ones. Much as I wanted to learn French, my brain needed a rest this evening. I wanted everything to be easy.

Hmmm. Let's see. There was a three-course prix fixe. Did I want the foie gras of duck with toasted country bread for an appetizer? Or how about their famous oysters. Maybe the watercress soup with Iberico de Bellota ham—whatever that was—and whipped cream. A soup with whipped cream couldn't be all bad. I should try their oysters. For the main course, I could have the chef's famous Indian curry, but that seemed a bit much for a July night. There was Red Label chicken from the Landes region served with carnaroli risotto with vegetables, but the only words I understood were chicken, risotto, and vegetables. There was also charolais beef tartare with French fries and a salad. Maybe. Or Norwegian salmon *a la plancha* with zucchini sautéed in lemon thyme.

"Gini," I said, "help me out here. What does 'a la plancha' mean?"

"Literally, cooked on a metal plate," Gini said. "It just means grilled."

Sounded good. Salmon for me. And, finally, what did I want for dessert? Apricot coup with mascarpone ice cream didn't appeal. Floating island and sliced almonds was okay. But grand vintage Guanaja soft-cooked chocolate cake was the winner. I'll take chocolate over everything else every time.

We gave the waiter our orders.

"May I offer you some wine?" he said.

We all looked at Gini. "Go ahead, Gini," Tina said. "Let's splurge and get both a white and a red."

Gini looked at the wine menu and chose a

Riesling for the white and a cabernet for the red.

We alternated between catching up with each other and people watching until Tina tapped on her glass to get our attention.

"So what do we think, gang?" Tina said. "What travel tips should I give my readers when I get back?"

"Don't ask anybody about his missing earring," I said. "Just ignore it."

Much laughter from my friends. "What else?" Tina said. "Some tips I can actually use, please."

"One thing you should tell them that I think is crucial," Pat said. "Flights to Paris in the summer are very expensive because it's tourist season. The French have all gone south and left the city to foreigners. So it's important to book your flight in February or March to get the best buys."

"Good one, Pat," Tina said. "That applies to hotels too if you want to get a room you can afford that's fairly decent. Book early because the best ones are gone by the summer. Most people can't afford the really expensive hotels on the Champs Élysées and the avenues around it."

"The best thing about coming here in July is the sales," Mary Louise said. "Remember that day we went shopping at the Galeries Lafayette and Le Bon Marché, Tina? Some of the clothes— even the designer clothes—were eighty percent off. And they were gorgeous. I wish I'd bought more."

"I do too," Tina said. "That's a really good tip. Oh, and Mary Louise, I'll also tell them the best time to buy is mid-July because the prices go down even more then."

"Oh, yeah," Mary Louise said, "and don't forget to say not to wait until the end of July when the prices are lowest because all the really good stuff is gone."

The waiter appeared with our meals.

One look at the beautifully arranged food on our plates, and all thoughts of travel tips disappeared. Even I was hungry. I can't imagine how I could have even thought of eating after my recent harrowing experience, but I dove in to my delicious oysters, slurping them down as daintily as possible, and enjoying the nice dry Riesling that the waiter had poured into my glass.

When we came up for air after the first course, Gini said, "Tina, I have a tip about the weather in July."

"Go ahead, Gini," Tina said, getting ready to make a note on her iPad.

"When I lived here, and up until recently, the average temperature in July was in the sixties. But now they seem to have heat waves when it's in the nineties. Must be global warming or something, but it's definitely much hotter than I remember. So you should tell your honeymooners to bring some cool clothes."

"Just don't tell them to wear tank tops and flip-flops and short shorts," I said. "There are still a lot of Parisians around who haven't gone on vacation, and they dress in sleeveless dresses and pretty silky tops and pants in the heat. You don't want your readers to stand out as crass Americans."

"Excellent point," Tina said, typing away rapidly. "What else you got?"

"Don't forget those sudden showers that appear out of nowhere," Gini said. "Bring a really lightweight umbrella that fits into your purse."

"Right," Tina said.

"How about some suggestions for gifts to take back home," Pat said. "I always need ideas."

"This is absolutely the best place to gift shop," Gini said. "Chocolates are always good. They make fantastic chocolate here. And gourmet food. It's everywhere. Oh, and a great place to find unusual things is a flea market. It's too bad we didn't get to one while we were here, but they've got great antique jewelry, old books, unusual scarves and belts and everything. We should have gone. And you can always find an unusual book in one of the stalls along the river."

"I would have preferred the flea market to being gassed in a room in a club," I said.

"Oh, Jan," Mary Louise said. "Are you okay?"

"I will be in a few years, honey," I said. "Don't worry."

My friends all made sympathetic noises, which turned into appreciative sounds when our main courses arrived.

The salmon was incredibly good, and the Riesling was perfect with it. I almost forgot my ordeal as I munched away.

While we waited for our dessert, Tina said, "How about a couple more tips and then I'll leave you alone."

"Oh, I've got one most people don't know about," Gini said.

"Great! Let's hear it," Tina said.

"A lot of stores are closed in July, but many of them post signs in the window giving you alternative places to shop. And by law—this is really so French—by law bakeries must have a sign in the window listing other bakeries that are open. The French have no patience with shortages of bread and pastries."

"Love that," Tina said, typing away.

"My friend Ken told me to avoid the long lines in the summer by going very early or very late to museums and other places you want to see," I said.

"I have one, Tina," Pat said. "Your honeymooners probably already know this since they're mostly young, but just in case, remind them they don't need to bother with a lot of maps because most phones now have a GPS that will tell them where everything is and how to get there."

"It's worth including, Pat," Tina said. "Thank you. OK, I think I've got enough for now. Let's concentrate on our desserts and forget work."

We lingered over dessert and coffee, sad that it was our last night in this marvelous city, but ready to go back home. I was especially anxious to return to a place where there was very little chance that anyone would try to kill me. I mean I live in New Jersey, for heaven's sake.

"Let's take some time off from dancing and murders when we get back home, Tina," I said. "I want to work with Sandy on the book she's writing about the Gypsy Robe tradition on Broadway. It's brought us much closer together."

"I think it's great you're doing that, Jan," Tina said. "I promise I won't sign us up for anything until you're ready."

"I also want to hang out with Tom when I get back," I said. "He told me about some plays he wants to take me to, and he found a new Brazilian restaurant he thinks we should try."

"Brazilian!" Tina said, leaning forward and grabbing my arm. "That reminds me. We have an offer to dance at the Copacabana hotel in Rio sometime in April. I forgot about that."

"You're kidding," Gini said. "Oh, Tina, I hope you said yes. I've always wanted to go there."

"I wanted to check with you guys first," Tina said. "Weren't you planning to go to India with Alex after we get back to find out about adopting your little girl, Gini?"

"Yes," Gini said, her face lighting up. "Alex has it all arranged. I was just talking to him about it on the phone before we came here tonight. He's been in touch with several government officials over there who might be able to help me adopt her. He wasn't too thrilled to hear about our getting mixed up in more killings, though. He said he was going to take me to India to get me far away from my friends who attract murderers like other people attract houseflies. He was really worried about you, Jan. He wanted to be sure you were all right."

"He's the neatest guy, Gini," I said. "Why don't you hurry up and marry him?"

"I just might do that," she said, smiling at me. "Wouldn't it be great to start off our marriage with a new little daughter?"

"We could take her with us to Brazil," Tina said. "Alex could come too."

"Whoa, Tina," Gini said. "We're a long way from making that come true. I told you how hard it is to adopt a child in India."

"If anyone can do it, Alex can," Tina said. "He's got *The New York Times* to help him."

"Cross your fingers, Tina," Gini said. "In any

case, I'd love to go to Brazil, whether I get to adopt Amalia or not."

"I might have to take Peter along," Tina said. "You should have heard him when I told him about the two murders here. He said he was going to handcuff me to his wrist so I couldn't go anywhere without him and get killed."

"Sounds kinky," Gini said, dodging Tina's punch. "You've been talking about marrying him for a long time, Tina," Gini said. "Why don't you go ahead and do it?"

"There's no rush, Gini," she said. "I do love him, but every time I get ready to plan a wedding, we go off some place to dance and there just isn't time."

"He'll wait for you forever," Mary Louise said. "He loves you so much." She paused, a wistful expression on her face. "Sometimes I wish . . ." She stopped.

"Sometimes you wish what, Weezie," Gini said. "That you weren't married to boring old George?" She laughed. "We could all understand that."

Tina saw the hurt expression on Mary Louise's face.

"Knock it off, Gini," she said. "George works hard, and he loves Mary Louise. He's not always the perfect husband, but who is? Even my Bill could be a little annoying sometimes."

"What about that guy Mike you met on the

train in Spain?" Gini asked Mary Louise, not getting Tina's message to shut up. "Have you seen him since you got home?"

Mary Louise's face reddened. She's the only person I know who isn't a teenager who still blushes.

"We've . . . uh . . . We've had lunch a couple of times in the city. It's nice to talk to someone who actually listens to what I say and who cares about what I'm doing. But we haven't . . ."

Pat, our voice of good sense, chimed in. "Mary Louise, you don't have to tell this nosy person about your lunches with Mike, or anything else for that matter."

"You did tell Denise about your French police captain, Pat," Gini said. "Wasn't she even a little jealous?"

Pat took a deep breath and held it. She looked like I look when I'm counting to ten and trying not to say anything brash.

"Of course I did, Gini," she said, trying to keep her voice calm and matter-of-fact. "In fact, I've invited Geneviève to come and visit us so I can introduce her to Denise. Now, drink your coffee and stop making trouble."

Gini laughed. "Sorry, guys. I don't want to leave Paris, and I'm being obnoxious. Forgive me."

"Don't we always, you rotten Hoofer," Tina said, smiling at her and offering her a bite of her chocolate torte.

CANCANS, CROISSANTS, AND CASKETS

I looked around the table at these good friends, each one so different from the others, each one of us willing to die for the others. We had survived another murder—well, two murders, actually—and another attempt to kill one of us. Surely, we would have better luck the next time.

Want to come along and find out?

ADAPTED FROM THE CHEF'S RECIPE FOR LAMB CURRY

4 lbs. boneless leg of lamb cut into bite-size pieces
4 oz. olive oil
3 diced Golden Delicious apples
1 sliced banana
2 tsps. curry powder
1 tsp. paprika
¼ cup shredded coconut
3 cloves minced garlic
1 cup chopped onions
½ tbsp. salt
¼ cup flour
16 oz. lamb or beef stock or water
8 oz. crushed tomatoes
Parsley for garnish
Bouquet garni
Mango chutney, chili, and achars as side dishes

Bouquet Garni
2 sprigs fresh thyme
2 dried bay leaves
Greens from 2 celery stalks
6 sprigs parsley

Place the herbs in a piece of cheesecloth and tie it into a bag with string.

1. Brown the pieces of lamb, one sliced apple, and the banana in the olive oil for five minutes.

2. Stir in the curry powder, paprika, and coconut.

3. Sprinkle with flour.

4. Add enough stock or water to cover the meat and spices.

5. Add the bouquet garni, season with salt, cover, and cook over low heat for one and a half hours.

6. Remove the meat and bouquet garni from the sauce.

7. Stir the sauce until it's smooth.

8. Put the meat back and simmer the sauce for thirty minutes.

9. Sweat the remaining two apples in butter.

10. Add the remaining two diced apples, the tomatoes, and the parsley.

11.Serve with rice, mango chutney, chili, and achars.

Acknowledgments

I would like to acknowledge the superb editing of Michaela Hamilton, executive editor of Kensington Books, who helped me make Paris come alive for the readers of this book. I would also like to thank Riva Nelson, who introduced me to some of the most fascinating people in Paris on my last visit there. A big thank-you to Robin Cook, the Kensington production editor who keeps making my books look irresistible. I am grateful to everyone at Kensington Publishing Corp. for their support in making my books so readable and attractive.

Don't miss the next delightful Happy Hoofers
mystery by Mary McHugh

Bossa Novas, Bikinis, and Bad Ends

Coming from Kensington Publishing Corp.
in 2016

Keep reading to enjoy a teaser excerpt . . .

Chapter 1

Welcome to Rio—Or Not!

When I told my friends in New Jersey that the Happy Hoofers had been hired to dance at the Copacabana Palace, in Rio de Janeiro, they said, "It's a beautiful city." Then they would add, "But be careful. Hold on to your purse."

I was a little worried when we got on the plane in Newark, but I figured I was used to New York, where I hang on to my handbag without even thinking about it, so I quashed my anxiety. I tend to worry too much about things anyway. I try to imagine all the bad things that can happen before I do anything and try to prevent them ahead of time. Of course, there's always something I couldn't have possibly foreseen.

I'm Pat Keeler, a family therapist, and I'm going to tell you the story of my adventure in Rio with my four best friends. We're a bunch of crazy, fiftyish in age, thirtyish in attitude tap dancers, known as the Happy Hoofers, and we were hired to perform at the luxurious Copacabana Palace. But our visit to Brazil turned out to be way different than any of us had expected. In fact, it was downright terrifying. We had been through some scary times in some of the other places where we've danced, but this one beat them all.

Gini is always trying to get me to relax. "You just can't predict everything, Pat," she says in her usual exasperated way. Gini is great. She's my favorite of all my friends in this dancing troupe, I think, because she says what she thinks, and is always honest with me. As a therapist, I'm used to people fooling themselves, trying to make me believe the illusions they foster about their relationships, so I cherish people who see life as it really is.

After we landed in Rio, on a bright April afternoon, we loaded our bags and ourselves into a black limo provided by the hotel. The driver, whose bright smile more than made up for his fractured English, pointed out local attractions as he took us past a beautiful beach that stretched for twenty miles along the coast of the city.

We were staying at the Copacabana Palace Hotel on Copacabana Beach. It really is a palace. Built in the 1920s, it was the place for movie stars and other celebrities to stay when they came to town. The hotel is pure white and seems to go on for acres.

The manager, Miguel Ortega, greeted us at the front entrance. He was good-looking, with black hair, dark, wicked-looking eyes, and a black beard and mustache surrounding a sensual mouth. He exuded a sexiness that was overpowering. He wore a charcoal-gray, expensive suit, and shoes that were definitely Pradas.

"Welcome to the Copacabana, lovely ladies," he said with a charming but slight Portuguese accent. "We have been looking forward to your visit."

When Janice, our actress hoofer, got out of the car, he ignored the rest of us and moved in on her like the ocean caressing the shore. "And you are?" he asked, taking her hand and kissing it.

"Janice Rogers, Señor Ortega," she said, pushing her blond hair back from her face. "Your hotel is magnificent."

"As are you," he said, unable to take his eyes off her.

A woman who had been standing in back of Ortega stepped forward and put her arm through his. "We are so glad to have you here this week," she said. "I'm Maria and will be your translator while you're here. I hope you will allow me to help you with anything you need." She was a slender woman in her early thirties, her hair in tight braids all over her head, her skin a pale brown. Her English was flawless, with no trace of an accent.

She gently pulled Miguel away from Janice and asked, "Which one of you is Tina Powell?"

Tina, a magazine editor and our fearless leader, held out her hand. "I'm Tina," she said. "We are grateful to have your help, Maria. None of us knows Portuguese, so we will rely on you."

Miguel tore his gaze from Janice to Tina and kissed her hand too. "We will do everything we can to make your stay here a pleasant one," he said.

Tina introduced him to Gini, a documentary filmmaker, Mary Louise, our only housewife hoofer, and me. He guided our group into the imposing lobby of this incredible hotel. Everything about it was grand. The lobby was huge, and the marble floors and columns gleamed in the afternoon sunshine.

"After you get unpacked and rested and have some dinner," Maria said, "I'd like to take you to one of my favorite places in Rio. I don't want to tell you much about it because I want it to be a surprise. It's a typically Brazilian experience."

"Sounds intriguing," Tina said. "See you later, Maria."

We got our keys at the desk and went up to our rooms.

When I saw the suite I would share with Gini, I was really impressed. It had a huge sitting room with a balcony and a view of the beach, an iPod dock, a widescreen TV, a fully stocked mini-bar, and Wi-Fi. There was a sleek modern bedroom with abstract paintings on the walls, an enormous, pink-marble-tiled bathroom with a bidet, a separate shower and bathtub, and a little kitchen dominated by an espresso machine. Gini and I grinned at each other when we saw our home for the next week. "Sure beats New Jersey," she said.

She went out on the balcony. "Oh, Pat, look at that beach! Acres of sand and water just waiting for us to dive in. Want to go for a swim?"

"Do you think it's safe?" I said, worrywart that I am. I try not to be one, but it's no use.

"Unless there's a demon undertow waiting to drag us out to sea, never to be heard from again, I think we're fine," Gini said, throwing one of the ten silk-encased pillows on her bed at me.

"I'll go ask the others if they want to come with us," she said and left the room.

I unpacked and put my clothes in the drawers and closet. By the time Gini got back into the room, I had slithered into my two-piece, black bathing suit, which, I have to say, really showed off my dancer-slim, flat-stomached, terrific-legged figure. Tap dancing will do that for you.

"Way to go, Pat," Gini said. "That bikini is perfect for you."

"Come on, Gini," I said, embarrassed. "You're the one with the big boobs. Are the others coming?"

"No, they wanted to rest for a while."

"They don't have your energy, Gini," I said. "But then—who does?"

"Too little time, too much to do," she said, putting on her own swimsuit, which proved my point. "I want a swim first."

We threw shirts over our suits and grabbed some sunblock, dark glasses, and towels and headed for the elevator.

As we walked out onto the beach, which was crowded with sun worshippers, we felt over-dressed. Others on the beach wore string bikinis and thongs that were so tiny, our swimsuits felt like granny gowns by comparison. The sun blazed down on us. It felt like it was about ninety degrees, so the thought of the cooling ocean was enticing. The sand was gleaming white and clean. We dropped our towels near the water's edge and ran into the sea.

The tide was going out, so we had to push our way through the shallow waves for a short dis-tance before it was deep enough to swim. The water was cool, not icy cold the way it is on Cape Cod at home. I swam out to where it was deeper, taking long strokes, not having to kick my legs very hard because the sea pushed me along. It felt glorious.

Gini caught up with me before long. Her style involved shorter strokes and faster leg move-ments, just like her personal style on shore. We swam along together in the salty water, looking up occasionally, long enough to smile at each other.

Gini turned over on her back and kicked her legs. "Is this great or what?" she said.

I rolled over onto my back too and did the backstroke.

"How did we get so lucky, Gini?" I asked. "We're in Rio, getting paid to be here, and swimming off one of the best beaches in the world. We must be doing something right."

"Maybe God likes dancers," she said. "Maybe he wishes there were more of us, so he does things like this to encourage others."

I'm not always sure there's a God up there helping us along, but I felt too blessed to argue with her.

"Race you back to shore," I said, turning toward the beach.

We kept even until the very last lap, when Gini passed me with a burst of energy, ran up on the sand, and flopped down on her towel. A trio of tanned teenagers interrupted their Frisbee game long enough to admire her.

I shook myself when I came out of the water and spattered droplets all over my competitive friend. "You always have to win, don't you?" I asked.

"Second best is no good," she said, drying her red hair.

"You should know," I said. "You're definitely a winner, Gini."

She made a face and said, "I wish. But I keep trying."

I lay back on my towel to soak in some sun when a man and a woman stopped in front of us.

"Are you two of the Happy Hoofers?" the man asked.

I squinted and shaded my eyes as I looked up at him. He was dark-skinned and sexy-looking, with a gorgeous body. So many good-looking men in this city. It was almost enough to turn me into a heterosexual. Almost.

The woman with him was wearing a barely visible top and a thong. Her large sunglasses made it hard for me to get an accurate idea of what she looked like, but her lips were sensual and shiny.

Gini spoke first—of course. "We are. Who wants to know?"

The man held out his hand. "I am Otavio. I used to be the bartender at the hotel. This is Yasmin. She still works at the hotel—in the accounting department."

Yasmin looked at us over the top of her Ray-Bans and said, "I'm glad to meet you." She didn't really look all that glad.

"What can we do for you?" Gini said. Her manner was not friendly. I was surprised because Gini is usually open to all comers.

"Nothing," he said, starting to move away. "I just wanted to introduce myself to you in case you wanted to see anything in Rio. I work as a guide now."

"Thanks," Gini said, "but Maria has planned our schedule while we're here."

At the mention of Maria's name, Otavio's smile vanished and his eyes narrowed. He grabbed Yasmin's arm and pulled her away. "Enjoy your visit," he muttered, clearly not meaning it.

When they were out of earshot, I said to Gini, "What was that all about? You weren't your usual warm and sunny self."

"I don't know what it was about those two," Gini said, sitting up. "There was just something about them I didn't like. And did you see his face when I mentioned Maria's name?"

"Yeah," I said. "I wondered about that. He definitely doesn't like her."

"I'll see what I can find out when we meet Maria later for our mysterious trip," Gini said.

"You'll be too busy taking pictures to ask her anything, if I know you," I said. Gini was devoted to her photography and was amazingly talented with her camera.

"Well, I'll try to find out about those two between shots," Gini said.

I picked up my towel and lotion. "Let's go back," I said.

We met our gang and Maria in the lobby.

"Please be our guests for dinner in the Palm Room," Maria said, gesturing toward a restaurant that was lush with greenery. "Afterward, would you like to see a side of Rio that very few tourists ever experience?"

"Always," Gini said.

"Meet me here at seven," Maria said. "Wear comfortable shoes. And be sure to bring your sense of adventure."

Pat's Tip for Traveling with Friends: Always bring earplugs, in case your roommate snores.

Chapter 2

Magical Mystery Tour

After feasting on partridge with acerola fruit sauce—divine!—we regrouped to meet Maria. She led us out of the hotel to a white van with the hotel's logo painted on its sides.

We drove through the main streets of Rio. Looking through the traffic, we saw a beautiful, modern city. People in bright summer clothing strolled the busy streets, vendors hawked their wares from sidewalk stands, and high above the city on Corcovado Mountain, the statue of Christ the Redeemer spread its arms in a timeless, benevolent gesture. After about fifteen minutes, our driver turned onto a narrow, dark street paved with cobblestones and stopped in front of a rather seedy little house. Its chipped paint and dusty windows contrasted with the gleaming glass-and-steel structures closer to the beach.

Maria led us into the building and down some stairs to a large basement room, where a half dozen women in white were dancing barefoot, swaying, their eyes closed, as a muscular, dark-skinned man provided a hypnotic rhythm on a colorfully decorated drum. Mesmerized, we sat on wicker chairs to observe the scene.

As we watched, one of the women went into a trance. The room was still as her body shook and she fell to the floor. For a while she was motionless. Then she rose up, opened her eyes and beckoned to Maria.

Maria walked toward her as if she were hypnotized, as if she had no choice.

"Your name is Maria?" the psychic asked.

"It is," she said, her voice a monotone.

"You are in great danger. Someone wants to kill you."

"Who?" Maria asked.

"I do not know. But I feel the presence of evil around you."

"You have to tell me who wants to kill me," Maria said, panic in her voice.

The mystic closed her eyes and fell to the floor again. She opened her eyes and looked at Maria.

"You have taken something that belongs to this person. You must give it back."

She slumped over, her head in her lap, and was silent.

Maria questioned her. "Who is it? You must tell me. What do I have that I have to give back? Help me." She shook the woman, who was limp and unresponsive.

Maria returned to our group, shaken and pale. Mary Louise, our mother hen, pulled a chair over for her to sit on and knelt beside her.

"You can't believe anything she said," she said. "She doesn't know you, Maria."

Maria shook her head. "These people have special powers. They can see things nobody else can. I believe her." She looked around at the rest of us, fear in her eyes.

"I'm so sorry," she said. "I brought you here because I thought it would be different from anything you would see at home, but I didn't mean for it to turn out like this." She gave a short laugh.

I wasn't sure I wanted to hear anything one of these mystics would tell me, but I could see that Gini was practically bursting to interact with them. As a documentary filmmaker, she's always looking for new subjects to explore. She had already made a prize-winning film about Hurricane Katrina in New Orleans, and I could tell she sniffed another unusual experience in this cellar in Rio.

Tina gave Maria a glass of water. "Are you all right?" she asked.

Janice, who was always up for anything that

came along, obviously wanted to be beckoned by one of the women in white.

The drums beat again, softly at first, then louder and stronger, rhythmically, hypnotically, and the women in white moved their bodies back and forth, their arms reaching up, their eyes closed, their heads turning from side to side.

A tall woman in the center opened her eyes wide and motioned to Gini. "Come," she said in Portuguese. Gini grabbed Maria and dragged her to the middle of the floor in front of the mystic. Maria obviously didn't want to go back there, but she was our translator so she followed Gini.

"I see you in India," the woman said. Gini gasped. She had just returned from India with her boyfriend, Alex, attempting to adopt a little girl she had met while filming a documentary on orphanages in New Delhi. Gini leaned forward to hear the mystic's next words.

"You left something there that is very precious to you," the psychic said, covering her eyes with long bony fingers. "You must go back and get it."

"Will I be able to do that?" Gini asked through Maria.

"It will be more difficult than you are anticipating, but you will be successful eventually." The woman turned away from Gini, and her eyes widened when she looked at Maria.

"You . . . ," she said. "You . . . ," and she fell to the floor.

Gini put her arm around Maria and led her back to us. "Don't pay any attention to her," she said.

"You paid attention to what she told you, didn't you?" Maria demanded.

"Well, of course. I want to believe her, but I—"

Maria grabbed Gini by the shoulders. "How did she know you were in India?"

"Oh, they probably have hidden microphones around the room, and they heard me talking about it before," Gini said.

I knew Gini hadn't been talking about her little girl in the Indian orphanage this evening, but I kept my mouth shut. How did the so-called mystic know? I mean, with all the places in the world to mention, why did she pick India? Listen, I don't believe in all this mystical stuff, but I had to admit things happen all the time that we can't understand. I try not to let that sneak into my therapy, but it's not always easy.

Janice didn't wait to be summoned. She walked up to the nearest mystical lady, whose face was gaunt and pale, and put her hands together in a pleading way. Her face is so beautiful, it's hard for people to resist anything she asks. Her perfect complexion and her blue-velvet eyes are very hard to resist. She never consciously uses her beauty to get what she wants, but almost everyone responds to her.

The psychic stared at Janice and said something to her in Portuguese. Janice realized she needed Maria and beckoned to her. Janice pointed to the translator, and the woman repeated what she had said.

"What did she say, Maria?" Janice asked.

"She asked if you would have a drink with her," Maria said, trying not to laugh.

I was close enough to hear this exchange, and I did laugh.

I should explain that I live with a woman I love very much—her name is Denise. I have always been attracted to women, though I tried to deny it for a long time. When I finally accepted this truth about myself, I found peace. Denise and I have been happy together since we met on a cruise in Russia.

The whole idea that this mysterious, mystical, eerie experience should turn into a drink invitation tickled me.

Janice looked startled at first, and then she smiled.

"Maria," she said, "please thank her for me and tell her I'm busy tonight."

Maria repeated the message in Portuguese. The woman looked disappointed, but she put her hands on Janice's face and said in English, "Beautiful. You will always be lucky."

None of us wanted to leave, but Maria gathered us up and led us back up the stairs and into the waiting car that took us to the hotel.

She walked with us to the elevator and said, "Meet me in the bar for a drink in an hour. It's beautiful late at night, and I'd love to know all of you better."

We went back to our rooms and finished unpacking.

An hour later we came back down to the bar, which lived up to Maria's description. Long and gleaming, with comfortable stools and elegant little tables near a grand piano where a man played soft, soothing music, it was the perfect place to relax and talk about our first day in Rio. We sat down at a table near the piano.

"I'm so glad we have Maria as our guide," Tina said. She was wearing a pale blue silky top and pants that made her blue eyes even more beautiful than usual. "She obviously knows Rio well and can take us to fascinating places like that weird house with those women in white. That was great."

"I loved it," Janice said, her blond hair swept back off her bare shoulders, "but I have the feeling that Maria doesn't like me all that much."

"She thought you were trying to steal her boyfriend—the hotel manager, Miguel," Gini said. "He zeroed in on you right away, and I saw the look on her face when he couldn't take his eyes off you."

"Oh, come on, Gini," Janice said. "He was just being polite."

"Yeah, right," Gini said. "Miss I'm-nothing-special. All men react to you like that. It's the only reason we keep you in our group. We get more applause with you there."

Janice dribbled some of her margarita on Gini's hair.

"Wonder where Maria is," Mary Louise said. "It's been an hour and a half since we left her, and she was right on time this afternoon."

"We should call her room," I said. "Maybe she got involved in something and can't get away." I pulled out my phone and dialed. There was no answer.

We listened to the music and enjoyed the quiet of the late evening when a plump little bald man who worked behind the main desk hurried over to our table.

"Are you the Happy Hoofers" he asked, an anxious expression on his face.

"We are," Tina said. "Is something the matter? We were waiting for Maria."

"She's . . . she's . . . the police have just arrived," he stammered. "There's been a . . . She's dead."